Alex leaned forward, and her full lips touched Jo's.

Desire exploded into a million tiny starbursts of sensation and Jo moaned as Alex's lips teased hers. When Alex drew slightly away, Jo's hungry mouth followed hers.

Jo felt as if she was drowning as the exquisite excitement magnified, multiplied, consumed her with a wild erotic craving.

Alex's tongue tip probed, and Jo willingly opened her lips. Alex's arms slid around her bare shoulders, pulled Jo firmly against her warm body.

As Jo's breasts touched Alex's, a shaft of desire shot through her.

Visit

Bella Books

at

BellaBooks.com

or call our toll-free number

1-800-729-4992

LYN DENISON

Bella
BOOKS

2004

Bella Books, Inc.
P.O. Box 10543
Tallahassee, FL 32302

First published 1997 by Naiad Press

Printed in the United States of America on acid-free paper
First Edition

Editor: Lila Empson
Cover designer: Sandy Knowles

ISBN 1-931513-96-1

For Glenda,
my **Little Treasure**

Acknowledgments

Many thanks to my friend Claire McNab, a top plotter, who encouraged me to try a romance for Naiad.

Thanks also to Glenda and Christine, who read the prototype of Dream Lover. I hope they enjoy this, the final version. And thanks to Barbara Grier for having such faith in women writing for women.

CHAPTER ONE

She lay on the bed, unashamedly naked. A cooling breeze slid through the open window and made the gossamer curtains sway in gentle undulations. She felt warm, secure, cocooned. She stretched languidly.

Slowly she moved her arm, running her hand over her thigh, her hip, her flat stomach, the small, firm swell of her breast. Her fingers stopped, teasing the rosy nipple that prickled to attention. She murmured softly, her hips arching as her body seemed to sigh.

She let her hand slide downward over her smooth skin, and it came to rest on the mound of soft curling hair. Her breath escaped on a broken sigh. She reached out across the large bed. Her fingers sought, and she thought she felt, the softness, the strength she craved.

Turning over she clutched at, merged with, surrounded that softness, and her lips moved in a satisfied smile. Her tongue ventured to taste, to sip the heady nectar.

Suddenly the wind gusted, swept the curtains aside, dashed them back against the wall, ran icy tentacles over her hot skin. She tensed, curled into a ball, buried her face into her sanctuary, but it had disappeared, lost again into the shadows.

Her cry of despair woke her. Mortified, she drew herself to the side of the bed, clutched at the sheet, ensuring it covered her body. She glanced agitatedly about her, desperately peering into the darkness, unsure of her whereabouts, and her mouth went dry with fear.

And then she remembered. She was in the Craven's flat just outside Montville. She felt her body beneath the sheet, found the familiarity of her old oversize T-shirt. Next she checked the bed beside her and saw she was alone. Her heartbeats tumbled over themselves, and she swallowed guiltily.

It was that same dream, only this time it was a little more vivid. Or so it seemed. Knowing what it was brought that same recognition of searching, of emptiness, and the same heavy sense of loss.

She couldn't pinpoint when the dream had first started, but she always woke the next morning and knew she'd been having that same elusive dream.

She was always filled with a faint sense of shame that she could be so wanton, followed, as she fully

2

awoke, by a sense of saddening loss. She knew she'd reached out for something, or someone, only to have them fade away at that last moment.

Jo drew up her legs, wrapped her arms about them, and let her chin rest on her knees. There was no point in seeking a meaning behind the dream again. She'd covered all that self-scrutinizing ground many times before, and she'd simply decided she was a psychoanalyst's playground.

What did the dream hurt anyway? It wasn't as though she ever found what . . . or who . . . she was looking for.

She flicked on the bedside lamp, which bathed the one-room apartment in a murky light. Perhaps she should get up, brew herself a cup of tea, but she was too lethargic to make the effort.

Jo sighed dejectedly. Things weren't quite going to plan. Being cooped up in the small flat wasn't exactly what she'd had in mind when she'd decided to take this much-needed break.

Unseasonably wet, the weather report had announced each night. The wetness wasn't even heavy rain like the thundering deluge of the summer storms. Rather it was an irritating, miserable drizzle that made it uncomfortable to venture outside without an umbrella, yet scarcely worthwhile using one.

Somehow she hadn't seen herself marooned with only her own thoughts for company. That definitely wasn't quite the antidote she'd decided she needed to pull herself out of the dreadful apathy that had steadily engulfed her over the past ten months.

Her idea had been to get away from it all, escape into the hills, do the sketching she'd never had time

3

for, try the watercolors that had been her passion in the early days. Before Ben.

So what had she been doing? She'd spent the week trying not to mull it all over again and again. Her life. Her failures.

And wasn't it just her luck to have a run-in with that strange woman on the first fine day she'd had since she came to the mountains a week ago.

The weak sunlight that morning had been like a sudden salvation. It sent her rushing thankfully for her sketch case, throwing it and a light picnic lunch into her small car.

It was still quite early when she'd driven around to a spot she'd noticed when she'd first arrived and taken a quick tour around the area. She was almost light-headed as she'd parked her car in a grassy lay-by and taken a path of sorts to get the best view of the Glasshouse Mountains spread panoramically below.

The group of scattered peaks, volcanic cores rising from the coastal plain, still managed to look majestic even from her elevated viewpoint. Their distinctive shapes seemed to have broken through, like islands pushed up from beneath the sea of green trees that surrounded them.

Jo sat on her small folding stool, resting her sketch pad on her knees. She was amazed just how easily it had all come back to her. Her eyes evaluated, composed, transferred the scene to paper, and she grew even more confident as she went from one sketch to another.

As the sun passed overhead and began its descent behind her, she lost all track of time. She was fascinated and totally absorbed, watching the colors change below her.

Eventually her rumbling tummy reminded her she was hungry, and she absently ate her hurriedly put-together lunch. She'd just stowed her water bottle back in her small knapsack when a deep voice coming from behind her nearly scared her to death.

"Just what the hell do you think you're doing here?"

Jo was sure she literally left her seat in fright. She twisted around, her heart beating wildly beneath her loose, pale-blue T-shirt.

She swallowed at the sight of the tall figure, imposingly backlit by the early afternoon sun. That the figure was obviously a woman did precious little to reassure her. Standing on the track that rose behind Jo only added to the impression of height, and Jo simply gaped at her in amazement. The woman had to be all of six feet tall.

In retrospect Jo decided her first impression was exaggerated, that the other woman was probably only about five-eight or so, but she was tall nonetheless, taller than Jo's five feet four inches.

However, taken aback as she was, Jo continued to stare in wide-eyed dismay, her gaze gradually taking in the other woman, section by impressive section.

The woman wore sturdy running shoes on feet set firmly, aggressively apart, and her legs were long, bare, and nicely tanned. She had on white canvas shorts, the cuffs rolled up to mid thigh, and a black T-shirt with white, stark silhouettes of palm trees splashed across the front. Her hands, resting

5

antagonistically on her hips, only accentuated her surprisingly narrow waist. Her shoulders were square, swimmer's shoulders, and the thin material of her shirt fell loosely over full breasts, which made it more than obvious she wasn't wearing a bra.

For some obscure reason Jo was reminded of the paintings by the old masters, of naked, voluptuous, so feminine bodies . . . She felt herself flush.

Her eyes, narrowed against the sun, reached the other woman's face. When she tried to swallow she found her throat had dried, her breath caught somewhere in her chest.

Framed by short dark hair, that face wasn't a conventional one, the kind men said could stop them dead in their tracks, but it was certainly striking. Perhaps it was a trick of the light, but Jo was left with an impression of strength. Angularity. As though her face had been uncompromisingly yet lovingly cut from stone. And at that particular moment it gave off an unyielding arrogance.

"Well? What are you doing here?" the deep voice prompted, and Jo forced her still wobbly legs to take her weight as she stood to face the arresting woman.

"Sketching," Jo managed, her own voice slightly high in her apprehension. "The scene." She indicated the view with a halfhearted sweep of her arm.

Oh, really gauche, Jo, she berated herself. You *are* the meek little mouse Ben always said you were. You've allowed this person to put you on the wrong foot without even attempting to make your own stand.

"I can see what you're doing." The other woman's full lips quirked wryly. "What I want to know is why? Didn't you read the signs?" Her deep voice had

6

a liquid quality, a huskiness that could have been theatrical but that Jo knew instinctively was genuine. "This is private property and you're trespassing."

"I didn't know. I mean, I didn't think anyone would mind. I'm sorry." Jo finished lamely.

A mousy little wimp. She could hear Ben's spiteful words, and she straightened and lifted her chin.

"I really didn't see any signs. I was just so happy to have a fine day to come up here. I'm —" She swallowed again. "I paint. I mean, I'm trying . . ." Her voice finally died on her, and she felt her fair skin flush with even more color. "I'm sorry I trespassed," she said with a little more firmness. "I'll just pack up my things and go."

She turned and began to collect her scattered pencils and sketch pad.

"Look, I may have overreacted." The deep voice, a little less belligerent now, halted Jo, and she turned back to the other woman. She'd dropped her hands from her hips, and she narrowed the gap between them in a couple of long-legged strides. "It's just that I have gardens and people think they can go tramping all over my property," she finished with less aggression.

She glanced at Jo's drawings, and Jo felt her muscles tense expectantly. She suddenly knew that same embarrassed urge to hide her work and protect her fragile confidence as she vividly remembered Ben's condescending indulgence that had finally killed any creative spirit she'd had.

"Not bad," the other woman said in that same husky voice, her dark brows rising as she looked from Jo's pencil impressions to the scene below. "You may as well stay and finish your sketches."

"Thank you." Uncertainly, Jo tried to smile, and the other woman stiffened just a little, dropping an invisible wall back into place between them. "I promise not to stray from here," Jo added quickly.

"Okay. Well, I'll be going." The dark eyes made one swift play over Jo's slight body before the woman turned and strode quickly back along the path and out of sight.

Jo lay back against her pillows and sighed. She should have asked the woman for permission to return as she wanted to do some more work on the scene before she began the planned watercolor. Perhaps in a couple of days she'd have the nerve to go back, take a chance on rekindling the woman's wrath.

She shivered and then groaned softly. What a fainthearted little namby-pamby she was. She had no backbone. She allowed everyone to walk all over her. Ben was right.

No! she told herself. Ben wasn't right. She was, had always been, considerate of other people's feelings. That didn't mean she was unassertive. If she felt strongly about something she'd say so.

Jo almost laughed. Who was she kidding? She'd been painfully reserved when she'd met and married Ben. Then he'd gradually taken her over, told her what to do, what to think. And that realization had only come slowly and painfully over the past lonely, stressful months. Since Ben had decided their ten-year-old marriage was finished.

How she'd loved him. Or thought she had. Now she wondered if any of it had been real.

Love. One syllable. Four letters. A small word

with such a multitude of meanings. Meanings so maligned.

Familiar waves of depression began to wash over her, and she squeezed her eyes tightly closed against the tears that welled. She refused to allow them to fall. She wasn't going to waste any more time weeping over something she had no power to change. After all, it wasn't as though she was crying over losing Ben.

She had to admit that it was something of a relief to be free of his manipulative personality. Grieving over her broken marriage was not the object of this exercise. The idea was to get herself together, to go on with her life.

Yes, it had been quite a day. First she'd met that striking woman, and now she'd had the dream again. And she was suddenly filled with the impression that the two were connected in some way.

The hair on Jo's arms stood up, and she shivered. That was ridiculous. What could have possessed her to think —? Then the woman's face slipped into her mind with such vivid clarity that Jo could almost smell the faint muskiness of her perfume.

She must be popular with the opposite sex. The thought came out of nowhere, and Jo felt the heat of color in her cheeks. But it was true.

Men would fall all over her. She exuded that unconscious aura of sexuality that seemed to come naturally to some women. With her clear olive skin and full sultry lips coupled with that deep, liquid voice, well, she wouldn't find it difficult to attract guys.

And even though her size was a little unfashionable, she certainly had all those curves in the right places. No, she wouldn't go short of male companionship.

Jo almost laughed at herself. Companionship? How prosaic. Let's not be so formal. She'd have plenty of bedmates. And Jo was convinced they wouldn't go away unsatisfied, the way Ben had.

She caught her bottom lip between her teeth. Comparing her lacking self with this attractive woman wouldn't help her cause. Yet it didn't stop Jo envying the woman her so obvious charms.

She reached over and switched out the light, but it was some time before she drifted off into an uneasy sleep.

The next morning Jo had arranged to take her landlady shopping.

The Cravens were friends of Jo's parents, and when Jo's mother had mentioned the flat attached to the Cravens' house in Montville, Jo had made an uncharacteristically sudden decision to ask the Cravens if she could rent it from them.

Her parents, especially her mother, had been devastated when Jo told them she and Ben had decided to divorce. They couldn't understand it, of course, and Jo had only given them the barest of details, that they had found they had simply drifted apart.

So upset was Jo's mother that she had wanted to

postpone their proposed trip to visit Jo's brother and his family in London.

Jo had adamantly assured her mother she would be fine, that she would be taking a holiday, and it was only knowing her daughter would be under Molly Craven's watchful eye that had finally persuaded Jo's mother to leave for the UK as planned.

Molly Craven took her responsibility very seriously, Jo reflected with some amusement as she drove with the elderly woman along the curving road toward the small township.

The road followed the ridge, and she allowed herself occasional glances sideways at the wonderful views of green rolling hills that ended in the hazy blue of the Pacific Ocean, some thirty kilometers away. Jo sighed softly. That fantastic view through the breaks in the bushy trees would lift anyone's spirits.

The small village of Montville could have graced the front of any picture postcard. The main street was lined with quaint little shops, galleries, a grocery store, and gas station. Flowers added splashes of vibrant, variegated color, and most days of the week one could see tourists exclaiming over the town's beauty.

Jo smiled with delight every time she drove through the village, and she did so again today. They passed the main commercial center and came down the hill past the windmill to a second group of picturesque cottagelike shops set among flowering gardens and lush trees.

Jo wanted to choose a birthday gift for her sister-in-law, and Mrs. Craven was only too pleased to have a chance to browse in the craft shop with Jo.

11

Parking the car beneath a tree, Jo hurried around to help the old woman out of the passenger seat.

They walked into the shop and began to pick their way between the shelves and counters covered in beautifully handcrafted merchandise. Jo smiled as she drew in the aroma of mixed potpourri and naturally scented soaps.

Her sister-in-law wasn't a difficult person to choose a present for. Kate loved natty things she could use, and for such a gift this place was a veritable treasure trove. Jo settled on a beautiful cross-stitch hand towel, and then she noticed a small stand of colorful handmade cards, deciding that would be just the thing to complement the gift.

Someone had used original colored photographs to feature on the cards and then inscribed them in an exquisite calligraphy. Jo picked up a card and turned it over. A. M. Farmer.

She looked through them all, wavering between a view of the sea in the early morning light and a close-up of a large honeybee about to alight on the pompomlike flower of a red callistemon.

"I'd buy them both. You never know when you'll need a nice card," said a deep voice. Jo started, glancing around to see the striking woman from her sketching expedition yesterday morning.

CHAPTER TWO

"Oh. Hello." Jo knew she was blushing. "I have a hard time making a decision if there's a choice. They're all so beautiful, aren't they?"

The full lips lifted at the corners. "Very nice." The other woman paused just slightly. "Who's the card for?" she asked casually.

"My sister-in-law," Jo told her. "It's her birthday. I've chosen this lovely hand towel for her, and I know she'll appreciate one of these cards. I'm a bit restricted as to what I buy as Kate and Josh live in the UK and the postage can be prohibitive if I'm not careful." Jo stopped and bit her lip, realizing she was babbling. "But I think she'll like this hand towel," she finished, a little disconcerted by the other woman's level gaze.

"I'm sure she will," the woman said easily.

"Do you think I should choose the one with the flower or the one with the seascape?" Jo held them out and watched as the woman's dark eyes went from the gift to the cards as she considered.

"Perhaps the flower," the woman said, and Jo nodded.

"I think you're right. But I'm also going to take your advice and buy a couple. I might even keep them for myself. They're nice enough to frame." Jo was sure she saw soft color rise beneath the woman's dark skin, and she watched a small smile play around the woman's mouth again.

Strange, Jo had never even considered the shape of anyone's mouth before, let alone a woman's. She was so close she could see each fine line, the raised lighter ridge that outlined the perfect shape.

The woman wore no makeup, but then she didn't need to, Jo acknowledged. Her skin was clear and had that healthy glow of someone who ate, slept, and exercised sensibly.

Jo's gaze dropped quickly over the rest of the woman, and she now realized she had a black leather jacket draped over her arm and her loose white T-shirt and faded jeans once again hugged her generous figure. Jo swallowed a sudden breathlessness and she shifted, unconsciously taking a half step away from the other woman.

"Well, I'll leave you to it," the woman said and went to turn away.

"Oh, by the way," Jo put in hurriedly. She went to touch the woman's arm and then as quickly let her hand fall. "I was wondering if it would be all right if I went back to finish my sketches? I meant to ask you yesterday but," Jo paused, "but I forgot." Or I was too taken aback, Jo added to herself. "A couple of days more should see me finished, and I promise I'll stay on the track." Jo stopped and gave a tentative smile.

The shadow of a frown crossed the other woman's face, and her lips tightened before she shrugged easily. "Sure. Well, I'll see you."

Then she turned and left, leaving Jo wondering if she'd imagined those few seconds of withdrawal before the woman had offhandedly granted Jo permission to trespass on her land again.

Reflectively, Jo took the two cards and the gift across to the cash register and handed them to the woman behind the counter. The sound of a motorcycle engine made Jo and the shop assistant turn to glance out of the front window of the shop in time to see the woman sitting astride a medium-size bike. She had donned her short leather jacket and put on her helmet before expertly turning the bike and riding off toward Maleny.

"I see you've chosen a couple of Alex's cards." The young shop assistant was wrapping Jo's purchases in tissue paper.

"Alex?" Jo queried and the woman indicated the disappearing motorcycle.

"Alex Farmer. You were just talking to her."

"She took these photographs?" Jo asked in amazement, and the woman grinned.

"Yes. And we do a roaring trade in them."

"Oh. I didn't know they were hers. She didn't say anything."

"Alex is like that. Modesty itself." The woman gave a soft laugh. "But very talented," she added enthusiastically.

Jo raised her eyebrows. "She certainly is if these cards are any indication."

Jo passed the woman some money and the shop assistant's smile broadened. She nodded at Jo knowingly as she gave Jo her change.

At that moment Mrs. Craven bustled up to them and handed her purchases over the counter.

"Hello, Cindy," the old woman said a little coolly.

"How are you today, Mrs. Craven?" Cindy asked with a teasing twinkle in her eyes.

"Not too bad," the old woman replied levelly.

Jo watched this exchange with some bewilderment. Mrs. Craven obviously did not approve of the young Cindy.

"I'm ready to go when you are, Jo," Mrs. Craven said, and they turned and walked out of the shop followed by a laughing good-bye from Cindy.

Mrs. Craven gave an exclamation of disgust. "That girl! No better than she should be."

With no little effort Jo continued to walk toward the car without glancing back at the young woman. Cindy must surely have heard Mrs. Craven's comment, and Jo felt herself redden with embarrassment.

No better than she should be? Presumably the old woman meant Cindy played the field. As far as Jo was concerned, Cindy had looked unremarkably average to her.

She wore the patterned batik full skirt and matching peasant blouse that a lot of women around the district seemed to favor, and Jo had noticed she had three or four pierced earrings in each ear. Her bright red hair was pulled back into a loose ponytail and, although Jo knew appearances could be deceiving, she wouldn't have said that Cindy looked at all provocative. Yet, come to think of it, there had been something unusual, almost familiar, about her demeanor when they'd been talking about Alex Farmer.

Mrs. Craven was making tut-tutting noises again. "Honestly, I don't know. Girls were different in my day, I can tell you."

"She seemed a nice enough young woman," Jo ventured. "Very friendly."

"Now very friendly she is, that one." Mrs. Craven pursed her lips.

"I suppose she must be quite popular with the young men around here." Jo felt in her pocket for her keys and opened the car door for the other woman.

"Yes, well, the young men around here don't get much of a look in," Mrs. Craven remarked enigmatically as she climbed into the passenger seat and Jo closed the door.

She walked around and slid behind the wheel, started the car, and turned up the hill to the small grocery store. In the opposite direction to that taken by Alex Farmer on her motorcycle, Jo thought irrelevantly.

"The world's a far cry from what it used to be," Mrs. Craven reflected morosely. Jo hid a smile. The old woman sighed and patted Jo's knee with her work-worn hand. "You're a nice young woman, Jo, and I know your parents are very proud of you."

"Thank you, Mrs. Craven," Jo said, more than a little surprised.

"And seeing as your parents are away on their trip, I'm more than happy to stand in for your mother, keep an eye on you, make sure you're all right up here alone."

Jo laughed, recalling that her mother had said exactly that the day she'd reluctantly boarded the aircraft for London. "Thank you again, Mrs. Craven, but I'm almost thirty, old enough to look after myself."

"That's as may be, but I'd feel happier if your husband was up here with you. I can't understand you young people and all this taking separate holidays."

The smile on Jo's face faded. She hadn't as yet broached the subject of her marriage breakup with the other woman. Somehow she knew Mrs. Craven would not approve of divorce. She opened her mouth to try to explain, but Mrs. Craven was continuing.

"Do you know, Dad and I haven't been separated in fifty years, apart from that first year or so he was in the army. Anyway, that's by the by. All I want to say is that this is a lovely little place, Joanna, but let me tell you there are some strange people living here these days."

"There're strange people living everywhere, some would say," Jo put in lightly as she parked in front of the grocery store.

"Well, the strange ones are more obvious here," Mrs. Craven went on. "You take those two that live up the road, the ones who've opened up that restaurant. One of them's as softly spoken as a woman. It's not natural, you know, two men together like that.

And it's not how God planned it," Mrs. Craven remarked. "Not my God, anyway. I won't tell you what Dad said. It doesn't bear repeating."

"The restaurant seems very popular," Jo commented appeasingly as she helped Mrs. Craven up the steps.

"Nobody spoke about it in my day. Now they're as open about it as if, well, as if it was normal. The girls, too."

"Some people feel it is normal," Jo said, wondering why she was championing a section of the community with which she'd never had any dealings.

"I think it's unnatural," Mrs. Craven persisted as Jo pushed their cart along the aisle. "And what I feel I should say, Jo, is that you should be careful who you talk to. You know?"

Was Mrs. Craven referring to the young woman, Cindy's, sexual preference? Jo raised her eyebrows. Cindy certainly didn't look like the popular perceptions of a gay woman. She would have liked to ask the old woman, but her characteristic reticence, coupled with a sudden slight sense of uneasiness, held her back. "I'm here to relax," she said evenly, "and to have a rest, so I haven't really talked to anyone."

All at once, with that same startlingly graphic definition, Alex Farmer's dark face appeared in her mind's eye, and the feeling of unease returned. "Now, what else do you need?" she asked the old woman, a sensation of discomfort urging her to change the subject.

Mrs. Craven readily began to exclaim over the rising prices of foodstuffs, and eventually they made their purchases. When they arrived home Jo reached into the backseat for her sister-in-law's gift before she opened the trunk where they'd stowed their groceries.

"You didn't show me what you bought for Kate." Mrs. Craven eyed the package, and Jo unwrapped the hand towel to show it to the other woman.

"And I bought these wonderful cards, too." She held them out for Mrs. Craven to see. "They're handmade, and apparently the photos were taken by a local woman."

"They are lovely." The old woman peered at the cards over her glasses.

"Actually, the photographer was in the shop when we were there. Alex Farmer, Cindy said her name was."

Mrs. Craven handed the cards back to Jo. "Alex Farmer you say? The one who rode off on that big motorcycle like a man?"

"Her photographs make wonderful cards, don't they?" Jo remarked eagerly, and the old woman sighed.

"Are you sure Ben can't make it up here for a while?" she asked, and Jo was momentarily disconcerted by the sudden change of topic.

Jo swallowed, knowing she'd have to tell Molly Craven the truth. She might as well get it over with now. "Ben won't be joining me. We've decided to separate," she said quickly. "We're getting a divorce."

"A divorce?" Mrs. Craven exclaimed in horror. "Oh, no. Not you and Ben. But you were so happy."

"We just drifted apart," Jo said, setting the old woman's head shaking.

"I just don't know what the world's coming to. I've got two grandchildren who are divorced, and now you. Where will it end, that's what I want to know."

"Sometimes things don't work out. Ben and I felt we'd be better apart. Now I just want to, well, make a new life, new friends." She shrugged, and Mrs. Craven gave her a level look.

"New friends are all very well. But just you remember what I said, Jo, about being careful who you talk to. I don't think that Alex Farmer's your kind of young woman. She's not married, you know."

With that final cryptic comment, the old woman gathered up her groceries, thanked Jo for the lift down to the village, and walked back to the main house.

A few days later Jo again collected her sketch book and some lunch and headed back toward Maleny. She shook her head in exasperation when she realized that the closer she got to her destination the more she was expecting to see a motorcycle hurtling toward her.

She was being ridiculous, she told herself, but still she smiled happily to herself. At least she could go back openly now that she had Alex's grudging permission.

Alex. Strange how the name came so easily to her mind. Alex. She wondered what it was short for. Perhaps Alexandra. Yes, Alexandra suited the woman. Strong name for a strong woman.

Not like Jo. Very plain and unassuming, she'd decided. Joanna, her given name, wasn't too bad, but Jo seemed so, well, dismissive. For a dismissive person. The thought sprang to life before she could quash it, and she sighed. Why did it take so much energy to battle her lack of self-esteem, her lack of confidence?

Jo grimaced and took herself to task. No confrontations today. Today she was going to put all her energy into her sketching, and the rest of the world, including her troubles, could float in limbo. Today she was going to sit beneath the clear blue sky, breathe in clean mountain air, and look out at the marvelous view. And feel good about herself.

With a surge of positiveness, Jo parked the car in the lay-by and climbed carefully through the barbwire fence. She picked her way along the track to the spot she'd chosen before and set down her small folding chair. Taking a few deep breaths, she murmured appreciatively. This was definitely the place to feel good about oneself.

Some time later she shifted in her seat and evaluated her work. Yes, she thought excitedly, this was just the angle she was looking for. She could scarcely wait to begin her watercolor.

A feeling of well-being had seeped into her, and she knew that she had been right to come to the mountains to spend time renewing her flagging morale.

She was taking in all the serenity, this freshness. She was reviving. And soon, she told herself, she would begin to feel like her old self.

No, not like her old self. She wanted to feel new, a completely independent, self-assured, confident . . . Jo stopped her train of thought and sighed. She wanted to feel like Alex Farmer looked. That's what it amounted to.

Perhaps, she reflected happily as she sketched

with sure strokes, the fascinating woman might come along and they could chat.

She grinned self-derisively. No, chat wasn't exactly the right word. Somehow she couldn't see Alex Farmer doing anything as inane, as insipid, as chatting. Someone like Alex Farmer would talk, discuss, consider a topic.

She laughed softly at her flight of imagination. Why she thought she could evaluate Alex Farmer's character on two very short meetings and a smidgen of idle gossip she didn't know.

The woman had scared her to death and then merely passed the time of day with her. Hardly a solid basis for character analysis. Apart from that, Jo knew she wasn't in the habit of doing such things. Usually she simply let anything and everything float right on past her.

Maybe that was the trouble, she frowned. Perhaps she'd used that remoteness as a barrier or a way of handling the inadequacy of her life with Ben. For those ten years had been geared to highlight her deficiencies, culminating in her inability to bear Ben's child.

Jo hurriedly pushed that thought out of her mind. She wasn't thinking about herself. She'd been thinking about Alex Farmer, a far more interesting subject.

And she was interesting. Jo stopped sketching, wondering just why she found the other woman so intriguing. Because Alex Farmer was all that she, Jo, wanted to be? Jo sighed again. Oh, to be so vital, so impressive, instead of a pale, ineffectual person who faded so easily into the background, quickly forgotten.

Jo straightened her spine unconsciously. Negative again, she reminded herself sternly. She was unassuming because she'd allowed Ben to shape her that way. And she didn't have to play that role any more. She was free to be anyone she wanted to be and do anything she wanted to do.

At the moment she was a free spirit sketching a breathtakingly beautiful scene. She forcefully pushed away her rambling thoughts and gave her full attention to her sketching.

A discreet cough drew her out of her concentration and she glanced around, her surprise replaced by a spontaneous smile of welcome.

CHAPTER THREE

"Hi!" Jo beamed at the other woman, inordinately pleased to see her. "Great day, isn't it?"

"Not bad." Alex Farmer gave a crooked smile. "Seems suddenly brighter."

Jo had to strain to catch the words, wasn't totally sure that had been what the other woman had said, but she had no time to wonder at their meaning for the other woman had stepped forward and was looking at Jo's sketch.

"I'm just about to start my watercolor. Or watercolors, actually. I'll probably end up doing a few.

The mountains look so incredibly different as the light changes I can't make up my mind which shades to focus on."

Alex nodded. "Sometimes I sit on my deck for hours just watching the transformation. It's something of a time waster."

Jo waved her arm at the panorama. "You have this view from your house?"

"Mmm. From a slightly different angle."

"That must be fantastic. Have you lived there long?"

"About five years. May I sit down?" Alex indicated the grass, and Jo nodded eagerly, glancing at her wristwatch.

"It's lunchtime. Want to share my sandwiches? They're just salad, but I can unequivocally recommend them," she said with a grin, and Alex held her gaze.

"You're on," she said in that deep voice. Jo's smile widened.

"I've brought some spring water. You can have the cup, and I'll use the lid from the cooler bottle." Jo rummaged around in her small knapsack and passed Alex a sandwich. "By the way, I should introduce myself. I'm Jo. Joanna Creighton."

"Hi, Jo." Alex wiped her hand on the side of her denim shorts and held it out.

Jo's fingers were folded in the bigger hand, which felt warm and strong clasped firmly around hers. Memory tugged at Jo, surfaced somewhere deep inside her, but it was a transient thing and just as suddenly gone.

For some reason Jo was reluctant to break that innocent contact. But Alex did that.

"I'm Alex Farmer."

"I know." Jo smiled airily as Alex raised her dark eyebrows. "The woman in the craft shop, Cindy told me."

"Oh." Alex carefully studied her sandwich. "What else did she tell you?"

"That you made the cards I bought."

Alex made a face. "Just doing a little subtle merchandising."

"You didn't need to. The cards sell themselves." Jo watched the strongly etched profile of Alex's face, her straight nose, her full lips, her firm chin.

Alex took a bite of her sandwich, and Jo was almost mesmerized watching the strong white teeth bite into the bread. "Do you take all the photographs yourself?" she asked, her voice a little thin. She swallowed quickly.

Alex nodded. "I've collected them over the years. I have a darkroom under my house so I can develop and print them as I need them."

"Do you do black-and-white besides color? I love black-and-white shots," Jo told her.

"I started out with that and worked up to color. But deep down I prefer black-and-white, too." Alex paused and looked back at Jo. "I'd like to take some black-and-white shots of you if you'd let me."

"Of me?" Jo glanced at Alex skeptically. "I'd make a pretty dull subject."

"Why do you say that?"

"Because I'm sort of average."

Alex raised her eyebrows again. "What's average?"

"Well . . ." Jo shrugged. "I'm not tall and willowy. I'm hardly well endowed. And my features are only nondescript."

Alex laughed. "Now that's what I call really selling yourself hard."

Jo smiled, watching the laughter lines crinkle around Alex's dark eyes. "You should do a self-portrait," she heard herself say, and Alex looked at her, making her flush. "You're tall and —" Jo began and stopped just as suddenly.

"Hardly willowy, but I am well endowed," Alex finished with an amused grimace. "Nice way of putting it, Jo."

"Oh, I didn't mean —" Jo swallowed, feeling herself redden with embarrassment. And she had to force her gaze away from Alex's curvaceous form.

"I know what you meant," Alex said softly, reaching out to touch Jo reassuringly on the arm.

It was only the lightest of touches, but the feel of it remained on Jo's skin, a prickling yet pleasing sensation.

"My whole problem," Alex was continuing, "is being in the wrong place at the wrong time. I'd never have been out of work back in Rubens's day." She laughed. "I might just have been the world's most posed model with all my charms on canvas for posterity."

Jo laughed, too, just a little breathily. Hadn't she herself likened Alex to the paintings by old masters? Not looking at Alex, she passed her a bag of fruit.

"But seriously, Jo." Alex rubbed the apple she'd chosen on the side of her shorts. "I would like to do some shots of you. No matter how you see yourself, you have marvelous cheekbones and a sort of innocent look. What do they call it? Gamine?"

28

Jo gave the other woman another skeptical look.

"I'd like to take them for a competition I'm thinking of entering. In the portraiture section, so no displaying of womanly charms, well endowed or not," she added lightly. "Just head and shoulders. If you can spare the time."

"Sure." Jo shrugged again. "Whenever you want to." She reached into the bag for a mandarin orange, concentrating on peeling the fruit, not meeting Alex's eyes. She didn't want Alex to see how pleased the request had made her.

No one had ever shown the slightest interest in photographing her before, except on her wedding day, but that was simply custom driven.

"Cindy said you were very talented," she added as lightly as she could.

"Cindy seems to have had a lot to say," Alex remarked dryly.

"Well, not really," Jo put in quickly, in case Alex thought she'd been gossiping about her. Which she had, she acknowledged guiltily. "Are you a well-known photographer?"

"Oh, very," Alex said sardonically. She took another bite of her apple, casually wiping a dribble of juice from her chin with the back of her hand, and she indicated Jo's sketches. "And are you aiming to be the next Hans Heysen?"

"Are you kidding?" Jo laughed. "I wish."

"That's a start, so they say." Alex pushed herself to her feet. "Well, I'd best be off. I'm keeping you from your sketching and ultimate fame. Thanks for the lunch." She smiled. "And the conversation."

"That's okay. I've enjoyed talking to you."

Alex nodded, her face suddenly serious. "I guess I'll see you around." She took two strides up the track and then stopped and turned back. "You can come up here to sketch any time you like, Jo," she said with a little less than her usual assurance. Then she was gone, long legs effortlessly climbing the rise in the path and disappearing out of sight.

Jo gazed at the empty track, wondering what had caused Alex's uncharacteristic uncertainty. Surely she couldn't still believe that Jo would damage her gardens. She sighed, wishing Alex had stayed. Half-heartedly she packed away the remains of their lunch and stared out over the scene, for once unseeingly. She felt a heavy aloneness now that Alex had left.

Alex really was nice once Jo got to know her, and she was so easy to talk to, a trait not found in many people. Usually Jo found making conversation almost painful. She suffered agonies trying to find something to talk about. But not with Alex Farmer.

Jo sat back and suddenly felt a little embarrassed. Yet she couldn't have explained why.

Had she talked too much? She'd rambled on and even asked questions of the other woman. Normally she found herself flushed and tongue-tied with people she'd just met, especially in a one-on-one situation. In a group she could at least fade into the background and leave the conversation up to someone more loquacious.

But it had been different with Alex Farmer. Jo sighed again. How she wished she could have had someone like Alex to talk to before she'd married Ben. And afterward.

Jo made a derisive face. At least she could be thankful for one thing. She hadn't scared Alex off by pouring out all her problems.

Jo took up her pencil and began a fresh sketch. But Alex's face kept getting between Jo and the view. How Jo would love to be just like her.

Pipe dreams, she told herself.

Still, Jo reminded herself, Alex did want to photograph her. Unless she'd just been making conversation. Perhaps she'd forget about it. Alex hadn't made any specific time. And after all, what was it about Jo that would make an acceptable photograph?

She knew she had nice eyes, a smoky gray color, and her hair was fair but not quite blond. It did have a natural wave, but that could be more of a problem than an advantage. She was, as she'd told Alex, undistinguished and average.

Jo sighed ruefully. She'd best simply forget about it as Alex probably would. And suddenly she felt a great sadness she was unable to analyze.

Slowly she put her sketching gear away and, slinging her knapsack over her shoulder, she headed back to her car.

Jo spent the next few days experimenting with her colors. She'd been extravagant and had bought good quality paper that was ready to use. The results of her first effort, although not exactly what she wanted, surprised her.

On Thursday she decided she'd better drive down to Caloundra to the bank to pay her few bills and check that all was well with the tenants in her parents' house.

The weather was still glorious, so Jo slipped her

swimsuit on under her baggy cotton shorts and loose shirt. She'd combine the bit of business with pleasure and go for a swim.

Jo drove past the person bending over the motorcycle parked on the edge of the road before she realized that figure was Alex Farmer.

CHAPTER FOUR

With a rush of pleasure she slowed the car and stopped. Keeping a wary eye for other traffic on the narrow road, she backed up until she could pull her car off onto the grassy shoulder. She set her hazard lights blinking and climbed out to walk back toward Alex.

"Having trouble?" she asked as she approached the motorcycle.

Alex stood up, stretching her long jean-clad legs. "Damn thing cut out on me," she replied, taking a rag from the pannier on the back of the bike and wiping her hands. "It's happened before, and I thought I could fix it but," she frowned, "it must be something else this time. Not a motorcycle mechanic by any chance, are you?" Alex asked lightly and Jo laughed.

"Do they take gas and oil like cars do?" she asked with mock seriousness.

Alex shook her head. "Pity. Then my second question is, do you have time to run me back to the telephone down the road so I can call the garage?"

"I can do better than that." Jo beamed. "I've got a phone in my car."

Alex raised her dark eyebrows. "That's a trifle decadent, isn't it? Don't tell me you're a yuppie?"

"If that means do I have all the modern conveniences then yes, I guess I am." Jo headed back to her car and Alex fell into step beside her. "My parents were worried about me driving up to Caloundra from Brisbane by myself, so they bought me one for a combined birthday and Christmas present. My birthday's two days before Christmas, so I often get a combined gift."

"I suppose it saves everyone making two decisions," Alex ventured as Jo opened the passenger side door of her car.

"You don't see such practicalities when you're a child. I know I often felt very deprived."

Alex dug in the pouchlike bag she had belted around her waist and pulled out a small notebook. She slid into the passenger seat and picked up the handset, following Jo's directions on how to use the phone. When she'd finished she replaced the receiver and climbed out to rejoin Jo. They walked back to the stranded bike.

"Des, the mechanic at the local garage who's mad about these two-wheeled machines, says he'll be here in fifteen minutes. Luckily he's not busy this morning."

"Great. I'll stay with you until he arrives."

"You don't have to do that." Alex slipped off her leather jacket and draped it over the motorcycle. "I don't want to hold you up any more than I already have."

Jo shrugged. "I'm not in any hurry. I'm sort of on holiday."

"Sort of?" Alex queried.

Jo pulled a leaf from a bush by the roadside and drew in the scent. "Long service leave from my job. I needed to get away from everything for a while."

"Know the feeling. And this is just the place for it. You know, it serves me right." Alex indicated the motorcycle. "I was indulging myself in a relatively lazy day. I felt like a swim in the surf, and I was going to justify it with a visit to the bank in Caloundra."

Jo gave her an incredulous look. "So was I. What a coincidence." She grinned broadly. "Great minds must think alike."

"So it would seem."

"Want to come with me in the car if they can't get your bike going?"

Alex gave her a quick smile. "Want to come with me on the bike if they do?"

Jo swallowed. "Oh. On the bike. Well . . ." She looked down uncertainly at the shiny black machine.

"I was only joking, Jo. You can relax. Besides I haven't got my spare helmet with me. Apart from that, I have a sinking feeling there's more wrong with the bike than I hope there is. So I just might take you up on your kind offer if it's still open."

"Of course." Jo paused and gave the bike another dubious look. "I've never been on a motorcycle."

"You haven't? Then when this one's behaving itself I'll take you for a ride. The road from Maleny past Montville to Flaxton is real bike territory. Long, sweeping, and it has a good surface. Very exhilarating."

"I'm sure it is," Jo replied doubtfully. "I guess I've always thought bikes looked dangerous, like some of the people who ride them."

Alex chuckled. "You mean I look dangerous?"

"Oh, no. What I meant was all those huge guys with beards and tattoos." Jo stopped.

Dangerous? If she went by her instincts she'd have to admit that there *was* something dangerous about Alex Farmer. Not dangerous as in threatening, but perhaps in an exciting, out-of-bounds sort of way. "Of course you don't look dangerous," she finished quickly, hoping her uncertainty didn't reflect in her voice.

"Don't worry, Jo. I'm a very careful rider, and I don't take lightly my position in the scheme of things."

Jo made no comment, for just then a dilapidated tow truck rumbled to a halt opposite them. A young man in dirty overalls climbed down from the cab and strolled audaciously toward them.

Jo felt her mouth tighten. She wasn't overly impressed by the young man's obvious arrogance, the insolent saunter, the bold half-smile he gave Alex before turning it on Jo. His presumptuous gaze appraised her in a way she heartily resented. And there was something more in his eyes as well, something she couldn't quite identify but didn't particularly like.

He took a packet of cigarettes from the pocket of his overalls, flipped out a cigarette, and casually lit up. "So, Alex. What's the story?" he asked easily, exhaling a cloud of smoke.

"The story?" Alex repeated patiently. "That's what I'm hoping you'll be able to tell me, Des. You're the one who keeps assuring me there's nothing about bikes you don't know."

"There isn't. Trust me," he said cockily, squatting down beside the bike and beginning to fiddle with it, asking Alex questions as he poked and pried.

Eventually he stood up, crushed his cigarette stub beneath his heel, and gave Alex what Jo considered to be an unnecessarily long-winded and complicated explanation. The technical terms went right over Jo's head, but Alex seemed to get the gist of it as she asked the mechanic questions of her own. Then the bike was being hoisted onto the back of the truck.

"Right. Do you two girls want a ride?" the young man asked, and Jo bristled.

"No, thank you." She unconsciously lifted her chin as she replied. "I have my car."

"Okay. Suit yourselves." He turned back to Alex. "Give me a ring later, and I'll let you know the damage."

"Just keep the damage down, will you, Des. And when I'm a millionaire you can work on my stable of Harleys."

The young man laughed, and Jo grudgingly

admitted he could be seen as quite attractive. If it wasn't for his attitude. Then he climbed into the truck and with a crunching of gears drove away.

Jo and Alex walked back to Jo's car, and Alex glanced at her wristwatch. "Still want to go down to Caloundra?"

"Of course. Don't you?"

"Sure." Alex put her leather jacket into the back of Jo's car, along with the knapsack she'd taken from the pannier on her bike.

"Let's go then."

"I'm in your hands," Alex quipped as she buckled her seat belt.

"No need to panic." Jo grinned. "Like you I'm a very careful driver."

"I knew you would be," Alex said dryly, and Jo switched on the engine.

Did Alex mean she was boringly predictable? Well, Jo acknowledged dejectedly, she supposed she was, and she couldn't see that she'd be able to change that.

They headed down the winding road through a section of rain forest vegetation, and Jo forced away her momentary dejection.

"Is that guy, Des, always so, well, so blatantly macho?" she asked Alex, and Alex laughed.

"Always. He's young, still wet behind the ears, but he's a top mechanic. I know what you mean though. Tends to set your teeth on edge, doesn't he?"

"That's putting it mildly. I can't stand the way guys like him look women over so obviously, like we're prize cows or worse. They must know we know they're doing it."

"Now, Jo, maybe the poor boy just fancied you," Alex said easily, and Jo exclaimed in horror.

"You're joking, aren't you?" she said, and Alex laughed again.

"I'm afraid young Des fancies himself as something of a ladies' man." She paused almost imperceptibly. "And he sees some of us as a greater challenge than others."

"Well, I'm not interested," Jo stated firmly as she changed gears and maneuvered the car around a hairpin bend. The ground fell away steeply between the trees, and she shivered slightly.

"You sound as though you mean that," Alex remarked.

Jo glanced quickly at her and then back to the road. "I do. I'm not in any hurry to get involved with anyone. Especially someone as obvious as that guy."

"Ah." Alex shifted her seat belt. "Is that a case of once bitten?"

"You could say that," Jo replied softly.

Alex sighed. "Relationships run the whole gambit of emotions, don't they?" she said quietly. "Love. Hate. Pain. Ecstasy. Uncertainty. You name it. Part of the human experience."

"You sound like you're speaking from experience, too." Jo slid another quick glance at Alex. She was looking straight ahead, her profile making her expression unfathomable.

"We can probably all dredge up one or two broken hearts, don't you think?"

"How long is it since your . . ." Jo hesitated, remembering Mrs. Craven's assertion that Alex Farmer wasn't married. Jo glanced at the other woman's hands, noticing for the first time that they were ringless. "How long since your relationship broke up?"

"Five years."

"What happened?"

"We didn't see our lives continuing in the same direction. How about you?"

"Apart ten months after being together ten years, and the reason for our breakup was," Jo paused, "something the same."

They were silent for a time, comfortably silent, while they both examined their memories. For once Jo did so without her stomach knotting. And just as suddenly she tried to imagine a man who would forsake himself of someone as compelling as Alex Farmer was. She started to question the other woman further, but Alex spoke before she could.

"Let's change this depressing subject. Tell me about yourself."

"I thought you wanted to get away from depressing and boring subjects," Jo teased lightly. "You'd be more interesting. In fact I'd say it was a safe bet that your life has been anything but boring."

Alex remained silent, and Jo glanced sideways at her. "Am I right?"

"That depends."

"One woman's boring is another woman's high excitement, hmm?" Jo suggested and Alex smiled.

"Believe me, Alex, anyone's life is absolutely absorbing compared to mine, so I promise you I'll be hanging on your every word."

"Well, let's see. I take photographs. I enjoy riding my motorcycle when it's going. How exciting is that?"

"I've seen your photographs, and they're wonderful. As for the motorcycle," Jo made an ambivalent movement with one hand, "that I'm unsure about."

"I promise, you'll love it."

"We'll see." Jo grinned. "How long have you been interested in photography?"

"Since I was about twenty. I met someone who was a fantastic photographer and a great teacher."

Alex paused, and Jo got a confusing mixture of vibes. She wanted to ask Alex more about the person who had taught her her craft, for she sensed he was someone special. But she also felt a withdrawal in the other woman. Perhaps this man was part of Alex's broken relationship.

"It sounds so romantic," Jo said. "Living up here in this wonderful place, taking photographs and making them into cards to sell at the craft shops. Everyone dreams about that sort of lifestyle."

"They do?" Alex shifted in her seat.

"Of course. I told you I thought you were interesting, and your life really does sound so exciting."

"My ego's enjoying this, and what's more," Alex reached over and touched Jo's leg, "I think I'm beginning to like it."

A frisson of something bordering on excitement spiraled inside Jo and completely disconcerted her.

The touch of Alex's hand on her leg had been momentary and light, but Jo could still feel the burning impression of each finger.

They went on to discuss less personal subjects, books they'd read, music they liked, and before they knew it Jo was driving toward the coast and into Caloundra township.

Jo found a parking space, and they agreed to meet back at the car within the hour.

"That should give us time for a quick swim before lunch," Jo said. "If you still want to go for a swim?"

"Sure do. After that intermittent rain, let's take advantage of the sunshine while we can. See you in an hour."

And she was waiting by the car when Jo returned just over an hour later. Jo quickened her pace, part of her recognizing Alex's attractiveness once again. Alex was reading the newspaper, her tall body resting back against Jo's small blue car. Her tanned arms turned a page of the newspaper, and her dark hair shone glossily in the sunlight.

Jo sighed. Alex looked so healthy and vibrant. So totally in command of her life. A niggle of despair worried away inside Jo, and she forced herself to straighten her spine. Perhaps some of Alex Farmer's self-possession would rub off on her.

"I'm sorry I'm late, Alex," she apologized. "I got held up in the bank. Have you been waiting ages?"

"No, not long. And I hope you didn't mean literally held up in the bank."

Jo laughed. "No, but I suppose it would be a rather extreme way of breaking the monotony of standing in line." She unlocked the car. "Which beach do you want to go to?"

"Kings will be fine. And I thought we could get some lunch down there."

They drove through the rest of the small shopping area and down to the beach. The sea glistened in the sunlight, and the breaking surf streaked splashes of white in the turquoise water. Heads bobbed in the surf, and a splattering of colorful umbrellas and beach towels dotted the white sand.

Jo parked the car in the shade of a tall pine tree and turned to Alex. "Doesn't it look glorious?"

"Makes you want to dive right in. So let's do it." She climbed from the car, and before Jo had moved she'd pulled her T-shirt over her head and was unzipping her jeans.

Jo got out of the car and stood undecidedly. She'd been about to suggest they go over to the bathhouse, but Alex's disrobing had preempted her suggestion.

Alex looked across the top of the car and caught her eye. "What's wrong?" she asked with a frown.

"Nothing. I just . . . You're too quick for me," she finished weakly and, standing in the token safety of the open car door, Jo slid out of her shorts and gingerly pulled off her own T-shirt, careful not to dislodge her modest bikini top. She grabbed her beach towel from the backseat and wrapped it around her like a sarong before locking the car and a little self-consciously joining Alex on the grassy footpath.

Alex stood in her one-piece black swimsuit, her towel clasped in her hand, and Jo's breath caught in her throat. The other woman was so genuinely unaware of her body that Jo felt strangely confused, and filled with more than a little awe.

Alex's body was in perfect proportion, and beside her Jo felt pale and anemic and decidedly lacking. If

43

she were a man she'd want to bury herself in that sensual body. Without warning, a fluttering of desire blossomed in the pit of her stomach and she tensed in astonishment.

Her mouth went suddenly dry, and she found it difficult to swallow. Then to her embarrassment she looked up to discover that Alex Farmer was watching her, her dark eyes seeming to see down into Jo's very soul.

CHAPTER FIVE

The other woman raised her eyebrows, and Jo felt her color rise painfully. "I'm sorry. I didn't mean to stare. I was just —"

"Just?" Alex prompted with a half smile.

"Just wishing I looked like you."

Alex laughed then. "Oh, no you don't. Come with me sometime when I try to buy clothes. If I find jeans that fit my hips, the waist is too big. If the waist fits, I have to pour the rest of me in. You can hear the seams screaming out for mercy as they prepare to split from stem to stern. And as for my top, what was it you called me? Well-endowed, wasn't it? Sometimes when I'm lying on my back I feel like they're coming to get me."

Jo giggled. "Sounds like a new slant on the old *Attack of the Killer Tomatoes*."

They both dissolved into laughter until eventually Alex took Jo's arm. "Come on. Let's hit the surf before we're too exhausted from laughing."

They enjoyed the cooling water and, having worked up an appetite, they sat in the shade of the palmlike fronds of a pandanus tree and ate hamburgers and fresh fruit.

"This is really decadent." Jo laughed, using her tongue to try to catch the dollop of sauce that was threatening to run between her fingers. "Maybe we should have chosen a sedate sandwich?"

"Not half as much fun," Alex said, and she reached across with the edge of her towel to wipe a speck of sauce from Jo's chin.

For some absurd reason Jo felt the warmth of color wash her face, and she rubbed at the spot with the back of her hand. "Delicious but messy," she agreed quickly and turned to watch the water. Just at that moment she was somehow fearful of meeting Alex's gaze.

When they finished lunch they climbed into the car and headed into the mountains, traveling in an easy mixture of silence and light conversation.

"You'll have to give me directions to your place," Jo said as she took the road to Maleny. "Although I didn't notice a house nearby, I know it must be somewhere near where I did my sketching because you walked there." She shot an amused glance at

Alex. "Unless you're one of those disgustingly healthy types who walks ten miles a day."

Alex grimaced. "Not ten. A couple maybe. And only two or three times a week. My place isn't far past the lay-by where you parked your car. It's fairly secluded."

Jo slowed down as she passed the lay-by.

"See the two white posts up ahead? And don't get a fright. The driveway's pretty steep."

Jo flicked on her indicators and turned between the posts, catching her breath as the car seemed to hover over a precipitous drop. Slowly she steered the car down the steep slope, but when the driveway curved to the right it flattened out.

"Wow!" Jo breathed. "This is fantastic."

The timber house stood on huge thick posts and was built into the side of the hill, the roofline a study in sharp angles.

"Isn't it what they call a pole house?" Jo asked, and Alex nodded.

"I wanted the house built up here to take advantage of the view, so the pole-house style was ideal for this part of the block."

"Did you build it yourself then?" Jo was consumed with amazement. Was there no end to Alex's accomplishments?

"That would be stretching it," Alex replied wryly. "I designed it and then subcontracted the actual construction work. Some of the downstairs section still needs finishing off." She glanced at the time. "Want to come in and have a look around while I phone the garage?"

"I'd love to." Jo climbed out of the car and hung

the damp towel she'd been sitting on over the steering wheel to dry while Alex unlocked the door.

"I've always loved anything that isn't the ordinary rectangular box when it comes to houses," she told Alex. "I'd have really loved something like this when Ben and I bought our house, but of course we ended up with something very architecturally mundane and boringly functional." She laughed lightly, but Alex had turned away toward the house.

She opened the door, and with a mock bow stood back for Jo to step inside. "Welcome to my place," she said easily.

The interior was all that the exterior promised. The polished natural timber floors gleamed, and exposed beams were featured in the high ceilings. Alex's furniture was rustic and comfortable looking. Bright scatter rugs matched the tonings of the heavy curtains that were drawn back from the huge plate-glass doors that framed the view of the Glasshouse Mountains.

"You do have the same view," Jo said in admiration as Alex slid open the doors and they stepped out onto the covered wooden deck that ran the length of the house.

"Aren't they amazing?" Jo leaned on the railing and gazed at the distinctive mountains. "I've been over to Moreton Island, and on a clear day you can even see those mountains from way out there in the bay."

They were silent for a moment, Alex half sitting on the railing, her back against a post. "Have you heard the Aboriginal legend about the mountains?"

Jo shook her head.

"In the story I read, the large mountain there is Tibrogargan, the father, and that next one is Beerwah, the mother, and they had many children." Alex indicated the rest of the mounds. "Well, one day Tibrogargan noticed the waters were rising, and he hurried to gather his younger children so they could flee to the west and the safety of the higher ground. He called out to his eldest son, Coonowrin, to help his mother who was with child again.

"When Tibrogargan looked back he saw that Coonowrin had left his mother and, greatly angered, Tibrogargan struck his son with his club and dislocated his neck. Coonowrin," Alex pointed out the sharp outline of the mountain, "has never been able to straighten his neck since then.

"After the waters subsided and the family returned to the plains, Coonowrin went over to Tibrogargan and begged his father for forgiveness. But Tibrogargan could only weep tears of shame at his son's cowardice.

"Coonowrin then begged forgiveness of his brothers and sisters, but they too wept. Tibrogargan turned his back on his eldest son and vowed never to look at him again.

"Today Tibrogargan still gazes far out to sea and never looks at his son, who hangs his head and cries, the stream of his tears flowing to the sea."

"What happened to Beerwah, the mother?" Jo asked, fascinated by the story.

"Poor Beerwah is still heavy with child because it takes a long, long time to give birth to a mountain."

Jo laughed delightedly. "That was fantastic," she said, and Alex shrugged.

"There are some wonderful legends from the Dreamtime." She stood up and stretched languidly. "Come in and see the rest of the house.

"The main bedroom plus bath en suite is up those steps. My workroom and darkroom are downstairs, and another bedroom and a bathroom are behind the kitchen and dining room. I tried to design the house so that every room took advantage of the view, which made the house long and narrow. But I do have the views."

Jo gazed around her with interest and then crossed the living room, her attention caught by a black-and-white photograph on the wall above the low bookcases. It was obviously Alex, a head and shoulders study, wonderfully lit to accentuate the striking planes and angles of her face. Her dark hair was a little longer, the style softer than the shorter style she wore today. Jo exclaimed with pleasure.

"This is wonderful. Who took it? Or is it a self-portrait?"

Alex came to stand beside her. For some reason Jo's body tensed, as though she was waiting. For what she couldn't have said.

"No. I didn't take it," Alex replied softly. "The friend I told you about who taught me photography techniques took it." She grimaced dryly. "Some years ago, I might add."

Jo glanced sideways at the other woman. A small frown shadowed Alex's brow, and her lips had tightened just a little. Yes, Jo decided, the photographer must have been the other half of Alex's relationship.

Alex moved. "I'd better call Des and see how he

50

went with the bike. There's some juice in the fridge, so if you'd like a drink just help yourself."

Jo shook her head and walked onto the deck while Alex picked up the phone. She rejoined Jo a few minutes later.

"Wouldn't you know it. He was held up waiting for a part to come up from Brisbane. I can't pick the bike up until after lunch tomorrow." Alex shrugged. "That's the way it goes I guess. So would you like to stay for dinner?"

Jo hesitated. For some reason she was loath to draw this day to an end. She'd had such a fantastic time. She felt as though she'd known Alex for years, even though she recognized that Alex liked to keep part of herself remote. And Jo could understand that. She was like that herself. To top the day off, she realized with a shock, she hadn't really thought about Ben at all.

"I'd love to, Alex, and thank you for offering, but my shorts and top are all damp and salty. I wouldn't want to sit around on your furniture like this."

"Have you got a change of clothes with you?"

"Only undies. I intended to change when I'd had my swim, but we seemed to forget, didn't we?"

"That's what we get for talking too much. You can have a shower here, and I'll lend you some clean gear. And I'll make you the best cold chicken salad you've ever tasted. What do you say?"

"Well, okay." Jo agreed with another swell of pleasure. "As long as you don't mind me staying."

Alex turned her and gave her a gentle push toward the door. "Go get your bag, and I'll find you a towel."

When Jo returned from the car Alex handed her a T-shirt and a pair of shorts. "These have a drawstring waist, so you should be able to make them fit. I've left you a towel in the bathroom."

Jo took the clothes and held out the T-shirt. "This is the shirt you were wearing that first day when you gave me the fright of the century."

Alex made a rueful face. "Don't worry. It's only me that bites, not the shirt."

"I'm greatly relieved," Jo said as she turned to walk to the shower.

"And Jo —"

Jo stopped and turned back to Alex.

"I'm sorry I was so rude that day," Alex said softly.

Jo grinned. "Apology accepted."

She stripped off her damp clothes and stepped beneath the cool spray, feeling it wash away the sticky salt of the sea. Moments later she realized she was singing softly to herself.

Jo tucked her legs up under her and relaxed back against the couch. "Mmm. This is the most relaxing house I've ever been in. It has a really peaceful feel to it, did you know that?"

Alex shook her head, smiling faintly.

While Jo was showering Alex had changed, too, and now wore a clean pair of white shorts and a blue chambray tailored shirt, the cuffs rolled halfway up her arms. Her feet were bare, and she radiated her usual good health and vitality.

True to her word Alex had fixed a delicious light

meal, and now they were sitting in the high-ceilinged living room drinking coffee. The last rays of the setting sun faintly highlighted the outlines of the mountains.

"Houses do have a feel you know," Jo said assuredly, perfectly at ease. "You walk in and you can sense it. Happy. Sad. Unsettled. I can enter a room and know if there's been an argument or tension. If it's strong enough you pick up vibes from the people." She raised her eyebrows. "You haven't had a blazing row recently, have you? I mean, don't leave me with egg on my face here," Jo appealed with a grin.

"No. No rows recently. It's a bit monotonous arguing with yourself."

"I guess so. But at least you could prepare a scathing answer because you'd know what you were going to say."

Alex laughed. "I suppose so." She took a sip of her coffee, and Jo sighed happily.

"Seriously, Alex. This room is so calming."

"Do you think so?" Alex looked around at the comfortable, well-used lounge chairs, the two bean bags to the side ready to be pulled up in front of the fireplace in winter. The bookcases along all walls, incorporating her ancient stereo outfit and television set.

"It's an atmosphere, a warmth. And you give me good vibes." She smiled at the older woman, who made a face.

"Now you're making me sound like a must for everyone's social list. Much more of this, and I'll have to keep you around."

Jo's gaze fell to the coffee mug in her hands as

myriad emotions stirred inside her, unfamiliar feelings she was loath to analyze just then. "I've . . . I've really enjoyed today, Alex. You're, well," she paused and considered.

Alex raised her dark brows inquiringly.

"Interesting." Jo shrugged in resignation and Alex rolled her eyes. "Well, no one could call you boring," Jo remarked with feeling, and Alex laughed delightedly, her strong white teeth flashing against the tanned, olive skin of her face.

"Thank you so much."

"I really do think you're one of the most fascinating people I've ever met. You seem very self-confident and accomplished. And nice." Jo stopped at the sound of the insipid term, and she colored a little.

"Nice? Meaning you think I'm a paragon of virtue? I've never been labeled *that*."

"I just meant, well, I —" Jo floundered, really embarrassed now.

"I'm sorry, Jo. I seem to be making a habit of teasing you. I'd be the last one to deny I have a few shortcomings. I have a diabolical temper when I'm roused."

Jo raised her eyebrows. "I know. Or at least I think I can imagine after having you accost me the other afternoon when I was sketching."

Alex grimaced. "I've also been known to overreact. On the odd occasion," she added with a grin that made her eyes crinkle at the corners. "I hope I can live that down and that I didn't leave any lasting scars."

Jo laughed, too. "Oh, just one. I'll never be able to sit sketching again without constantly checking over my shoulder to see if a ferocious landowner is bearing down on me, breathing fire." Her gray eyes met Alex's dark ones, held them, and something shifted in the middle of her chest. Her smile faded slightly.

"You should laugh more often," Alex said softly. "It changes your whole face. Makes you look younger."

Jo's gaze dropped again to her hands, and she raised her coffee mug to her lips. "Remind me to keep smiling. I need all the younger I can get."

"Just wait till you get to my age and you'll have something to complain about."

"Your age?" Jo mocked. "You sound like Methuselah."

Jo ran her eyes assessingly over Alex's tall body as she lounged back in her chair. Strong, tanned arms rested easily along the arms of the chair, one hand balancing her coffee mug. How old was she, this attractive, compelling woman?

Alex's face was virtually unlined but surprisingly, when you were close enough, you could see there were flecks of gray in the dark hair. And she had an air of experience, of assurance, that usually only came with maturity.

"Well, what do you think?" Alex's lips twitched.

"Think?" Jo stammered, realizing she had been caught. Transparently caught. "About what?" she asked guilelessly.

"About my age," Alex explained dryly. "Care to take a guess?"

Jo shook her head. "I don't think I'd dare. What if I said you were ten years older than you were?"

"Coward."

"I am not." Jo frowned in mock concentration. "And besides, you wouldn't like to guess at mine."

"Ah. A challenge. Let's see. Just going by the time factor and considering the information I have, you would have had a reasonable education. You said you'd been in a relationship for ten years. So, I'd say you were about twenty-seven or eight. You don't look it, but you'd have to be. Right?"

"Almost. I'm twenty-nine. Nearer thirty, actually. And I sometimes feel like I'm pushing sixty. So, tell me, how old are you?" Jo persisted when Alex remained silent.

"Your turn to guess. Just pick a number."

"Well, you haven't given me a lot of clues, but how does thirty-two sound?"

"Flattering," Alex said. "Very flattering for someone who's thirty-seven." She pulled at a strand of thick hair, and then patted it automatically back into place. "These premature gray streaks began to appear when I was about your age. I think I inherited them from my father. He was completely gray by the time he was forty. Very distinguished on a man."

"More double standards," Jo remarked caustically. "They sure have everything going for them, don't they? Men, I mean."

"Oh, I wouldn't say that exactly," Alex replied softly, her eyes twinkling. "Superficially, perhaps."

Jo gave an exclamation of disgust. "Well, I think the whole world seems to revolve around what men say and do." She made a face. "Don't mind me. I suspect I'm rather off men just at the moment."

Alex gazed down into her coffee mug. "Has that got something to do with Ben of the very architecturally mundane and boringly functional house?" she asked evenly.

Jo sighed. "Yes, I guess it has. It is all very mundane, but I think you'd say it's more boringly dysfunctional," she said with a humorless laugh. "And not a story you'd want to put yourself through."

"Try me." Alex set her coffee mug down on the table beside her and sat back in her chair.

"Well, stop me when you've had enough," Jo said. "It was the usual. We got married. Now we're almost divorced." She shrugged.

Alex was watching her, and Jo could feel her steady gaze. She made herself meet the other woman's dark eyes.

"No big deal," she added with a laugh that sounded forced to her own ears. She sighed. "Yes, it was. It still is." She grimaced, running her fingers lightly along the hem of the shorts Alex had loaned her.

"The breaking up of a relationship, no matter that it may have been unsatisfactory, is always traumatic," Alex said quietly. "Doesn't seem to matter how bad it was; the parting still leaves a void."

Jo nodded. "That's exactly how I feel. Sort of empty." She rubbed her forehead unconsciously. "It's not so much that I miss Ben as such. I guess I just miss the someone there." Jo gave a softly bitter laugh. "At the same time, it's a relief to be away from him. Ben was very," she paused, "very demanding, that things be just so. It really is kind of liberating to be on my own." She sighed again. "It's also hard to explain."

"I know what you mean." Alex's deep voice soothed Jo's sudden inner agitation. "How long did you say you'd been separated?"

"Ten months. And we'd been married for ten years." Jo made a face. "We'll be filing our petition soon, and hopefully we'll get a hearing quickly. I can but hope there won't be a run on divorces that month so it won't be long and drawn out. Now I just want it over and done with."

"Neither of you has wanted to change your mind?"

Jo shook her head. "No. Once the decision was made we stuck to it. Now we've been apart for ten months. If we were ever together, that is. In retrospect I have grave doubts. That's what happens when you believe in fairy tales."

Alex smiled faintly. "Those elusive knights on white chargers have a lot to answer for, don't they?"

Jo nodded. "You'd think if they knew there were so few to go around they'd stop advertising them, wouldn't you?"

Alex laughed.

"Sometimes I think my life's been a fairy tale in reverse," Jo continued. "The prince proposed and kissed the princess, and she went to sleep for ten years. But the past year has certainly waked me up. You know, I really believed in love and happily ever after."

"Don't give up on it. I haven't."

Jo's gray eyes met Alex's dark ones again, and a tiny shaft of pleasure raced through Jo. If she were a

man and if she was in love with Alex Farmer, she'd
have no trouble in believing in it, too.

A strange mixture of excitement and anxiety
churned inside Jo. She suddenly remembered her
reaction to Alex's body as she'd stood in her
swimsuit, and she found herself blinking in disturbing
confusion.

CHAPTER SIX

"There are some happy marriages," Alex was continuing as Jo fought to regain her vacillating composure. "My parents? My brother's marriage is reasonably happy. I have a few happily married friends."

"All the marriages in my family are happy, too. Mine going astray was a first." Jo shook her head, composed again. "I was so thick. I should have known right from the start that Ben and I were incompatible."

"You said you'd married young, didn't you? How could you have known?"

Jo sighed. "I was nearly eighteen, going on twelve when I met Ben. He was twenty-three, handsome, and seemed so self-assured." Jo gave a humorless laugh. "But who wouldn't have seemed worldly compared to the naive little fool I was back then? We were married just before my nineteenth birthday."

"So what happened?"

Jo rolled her eyes expressively. "The standard convention. Another woman. And as in all good soap operas, the wife was the last to know. I didn't so much as suspect." Jo raised her hands and let them fall. "Toward the end I even thought we were getting on a little better." She paused and slid a swift glance across at Alex. "And do you want to know the worst part of it? I was the one who felt guilty because Ben strayed. I suspect I still do."

"Which you shouldn't," Alex said.

Jo nodded. "In my rational moments I know that but . . . I blame myself when I know how illogical it is to do that." Jo swallowed, the familiar pain returning, a mixture of rejection and regret, of respite and relief. She felt her throat tighten with tears and fought for control. She'd hate to weakly break down in front of the other woman.

"Feeling guilty," Alex commented ironically, "now that's fatal. And I'm beginning to think that for women it's inevitable." Her full lips twisted mockingly. "Must come in one of our chromosomes."

Jo gave a small laugh and relaxed a little. "I think you're right. And some of us have more virulent strains of it than others. I know it mightn't seem like it, but I am coming to terms with, with everything. Slowly but surely, I hope."

"So. Is — what's-his-name? Ben? — Is Ben still with the other woman?"

Jo looked down at her hands and nodded. "Oh, yes. They have a child. A son."

"Ah."

Jo glanced up at Alex, color washing her cheeks, and just as quickly looked away.

"I'm sorry, Jo. It's obviously still painful for you and I shouldn't have pried."

"No. Yes. I mean —" Jo stopped. If only Alex knew it all. For some reason it was all coming out. How four years after their marriage Ben had decided it was time to start a family, although Jo had been uncertain the time was right. After two years they'd still been unsuccessful, and the string of awful tests had been taken.

"The results were frustratingly inconclusive," Jo said. "There was nothing physically wrong with either of us the doctor told us, and had we been married to different partners we probably would have each had a handful of children. The doctor suggested we put it all out of our minds, take a holiday and let nature take its course."

"And nature didn't cooperate?" Alex put in gently. Jo shook her head. "I'm sorry, Jo. It must have been hard."

Jo sighed. "More guilt," she said mockingly. "You see, I wasn't as disappointed as Ben was." There, she'd said it out loud for the first time. She hadn't even admitted that deep dark secret to anyone, not even her mother, and certainly not to Ben. "I wasn't sure," she looked up at Alex, "and I'm still not sure that I want a child. Unnatural and selfish of me, isn't it?"

"No. I don't think it is. Not everyone, and that includes men and women, wants children. And just being a woman doesn't mean you have to have a burning desire to procreate."

"I was terrified back then that I'd make a hash of motherhood. It seemed such a mammoth responsibility, raising a child, another human being. And if I did it wrongly, well . . ." Jo shrugged. "I'm a coward, I guess."

"At least you knew what being a parent entailed." Alex smiled faintly.

"I thought at the time my not getting pregnant when Ben wanted it so much was my subconscious taking over because I was so negative about it." Jo rubbed her forehead pensively. "It got pretty harrowing. I was always so tense." Jo stopped again and swallowed a knot of embarrassment.

She had been about to confide in Alex what a failure she'd been in bed. Alex definitely wouldn't want to hear all that. "I guess part of me can't really blame Ben for seeking what he wanted elsewhere." Where it wasn't such a chore, a strained duty. Jo looked across the room unseeingly.

"As I said before, I have this awful feeling that I spent the ten years of my marriage in a daze, an absolutely unintelligible dream. I was so bloody naive. If only I'd —" She shook her head.

"Oh, no. The dreaded *if only* syndrome. A close relative of painful introspection," Alex said lightly. Jo gave a weak smile.

"Pity we didn't get future-sight so we could prepare ourselves and sort ourselves out without going through all the dramas and traumas, isn't it?"

"But then what would we depend on to make better people of ourselves, to build our characters?"

Jo grimaced. "In my lowest moments I feel I've had so much character building I qualify for sainthood."

"Saint Jo." Alex gave a laugh. "And are you?"

"A saint?" Jo raised her eyebrows. "Are you kidding?"

"Sometimes you remind me of paintings of saints that I've seen," Alex said quietly. "Serene and ethereal, with your fair hair and big eyes."

Jo blushed. "Well, I don't feel very saintly. Unfortunately I'm just fallibly human, sometimes more fallibly human than others. One night we'd been out to a dinner party with Ben's boss and his wife. When we came home Ben was angry with me. He said I'd just sat there like a gawk all night with precious little conversational skills and looking like a wimp. For the first time I just lost my temper. Lost every bit of control I had."

"That must have taken him aback."

Jo gave a bitter laugh. "He got the fright of his life. He refused to speak to me for two whole weeks. When he did it was to tell me he wanted a divorce."

"Just like that?"

Jo nodded. "Just like that. He also told me he had a baby son. Now that took me aback." Jo took a gulp of her drink. "I didn't even suspect he was seeing someone else, let alone that he had a child," she said softly.

"Nice type!" Alex exclaimed.

"Remember I said I'd been in a daze for ten years? Well, that woke me up. I felt as though I was standing outside my body, that the two people I was watching were part of some heavy drama on television." Jo looked out into the darkness at the Glasshouse Mountains, but she wasn't seeing their almost undecipherable shapes.

"Snap out of it, Jo!" She heard Ben's voice from the past. "You must have known our marriage has been going bad. It's been shaky for years."

"I thought it was getting better," she'd managed to get out, and Ben had laughed.

"You're bloody delusional. We haven't even had sex for a month," he'd jibed. Jo had gazed at his handsome face, realizing she was looking at a perfect stranger.

"You must have been . . . You've been having sex with someone else while you were sleeping with me. My God! Didn't you think of the health risks you were taking? How many women were there?"

"You're overreacting. There was only one. Janet and I have been seeing each other for nearly two years."

"And she has a child? Your child?"

"Of course it's mine. He's three months old. And I want to marry his mother." Ben had had the grace then to look a little ill at ease. "You needn't worry, Jo. Financially I intend to do the right thing."

He'd had it all worked out, she'd realized later. And she'd made it easy for him by packing her suitcase and walking out.

* * * * *

"Ben and Janet and the baby are living in the house," she said aloud, coming back to the present at the sound of her own voice.

"I take it they're paying you for your half share?" Alex stated, and Jo nodded tiredly.

"Oh, yes. Ben continues to tell me how fair he's being." Jo rolled her eyes. "But this is boring for you. I told you it's the same old story."

"I didn't mind listening, Jo. Sometimes it does a person good to talk about it."

"I really haven't talked about it very much. Not in depth, anyway. All of our friends were sort of Ben's friends. At least I found out they were," she added dryly. "And I didn't want to worry my parents as they were going overseas. In fact, my mother only went because she knew I was going to be coming up here under the watchful eyes of the Cravens, who own the flat I'm staying in."

"Was that the old woman I saw you with in the craft shop?"

"Yes. They're really nice people." Jo shrugged. "But it's almost like being a teenager again and having parents looking over your shoulder."

Alex smiled. "So no riotous nights of wine, wild men, and dirty ditties."

Jo burst out laughing. "Hardly. Even if I could I'm a total bore. I think I'd fall asleep before I got drunk. I probably wouldn't know a dirty ditty if I heard one. And as for the wild men, well, I think I can safely say I'm off men, wild or tamed. So you see," Jo held out her hands palms upward, "it's

66

elementary. Jo Creighton, a sure thing when it comes to killing anyone's party spirit."

"Oh, dear." Alex shook her head in mock horror. "There's no hope for you then."

"None," Jo agreed and grinned. "A few months ago I wouldn't have been able to smile as I said that. Time must be healing my wounds, do you think?"

Or perhaps, Jo reflected to herself, it's just being in the company of someone new, someone at ease with herself. Someone exciting, her inner voice added, and Jo shifted uneasily in her seat.

"Oh, I'm a great believer in that," Alex said, and Jo blinked at her uncertainly. "In time healing all wounds," she repeated, and Jo exhaled the breath she'd been holding.

"Oh. Yes," she agreed quickly.

A sudden silence filled the room, and Jo swallowed.

"Well." She glanced at her wristwatch and raised her eyes at the time. "I guess I should be going. Now that I've talked you nearly to death." She stood up. "I'll wash the shorts and top and drop them back to you."

"There's no hurry for them." Alex pushed herself to her feet and stretched, the soft material of her blue shirt molding her full breasts.

For one long moment the bottom of the shirt parted and Jo caught a glimpse of the other woman's smooth midriff. She glanced away and began walking to the door, reluctant yet eager to leave.

"Thanks for the lift down to Caloundra," Alex said behind her.

Jo reached out for the doorknob. She paused and

turned back to Alex. "Thank you for your most enjoyable company. My turn to make you dinner next time."

"Deal." Alex smiled, the corners of her eyes crinkling, and Jo's own smile widened.

"Would you like a lift down to the garage to collect your bike tomorrow?" she asked, and Alex hesitated.

"Perhaps we could take those photos I was talking to you about the other day, for the competition, and then you could drop me down there on your way home."

"You mean you were really serious about taking my photo? I thought you were just, well, I thought it was a maybe."

"No. I do want to take some shots. In fact, they have to be done by next Thursday, so tomorrow would be great. I can have everything set up before you get here."

"What time shall I come over?" Jo felt irrationally pleased that she would be seeing Alex again so soon.

"Any time after lunch. How about one-thirty?"

"Great. What do you want me to wear?"

"Have you got a shirt with a neckline that sits about here?" Alex reached out her hand and touched Jo's collarbone, and Jo felt herself tense just slightly. For some reason she imagined she felt Alex's finger on her bare skin instead of her T-shirt, and her blood seemed to run cold in her veins. And then hot.

"I should have something," she replied a little breathily. "Dark or light?"

Alex frowned in consideration. "Lightish, I think. Although it's not critical." Her lips twisted wryly. "I could always lend you something of mine."

Jo laughed and looked down at the shirt and shorts Alex had loaned her. "So you could. Well. It's been a lovely day, Alex. And thanks again for dinner." Jo opened the door and stepped out into the darkness.

Alex reached behind the door and flicked a switch, the outside light wrapping them in a pool of brightness.

Jo turned back to her, eyes taking in the relaxed lines of Alex's body as she leaned one shoulder on the door frame. "Don't forget, I owe you dinner," she reminded the other woman and Alex nodded. "You can test my culinary skills next time. If you're game," she added with a laugh. "See you tomorrow."

Jo moved around the small flat fluffing cushions, shifting a small stack of magazines, straightening a pile of books. She stood back, running a worried eye over the room.

She'd thrown a bright picnic blanket over the couch that folded out into her bed. As a centerpiece on the small table she'd placed a bowl containing three floating scented candles and the subtle aroma of musky rose was permeating the air.

The meal was as near ready as she could make it and she was dressed.

She smoothed the folds of her dark-printed, full skirt and patted the neckline of her blouse. Should she change this plain white shirt for the more formal pale cream silky one? She took a few steps toward her wardrobe and stopped. No. The satin long-sleeve blouse would be too dressy for a casual dinner.

Casual. Jo caught sight of herself in the mirror on the wardrobe door. It didn't feel casual, and neither did she.

Uncharacteristic high color washed her cheeks, and her eyes sparkled with inner excitement. The tingling sensations of anticipation fluttered in her stomach. She felt like a teenager on her first date.

Jo sobered, a frown creasing her forehead. What was she thinking about? She was simply having a friend over for dinner. She'd done it before, played hostess to Ben's colleagues and his friends.

She was simply excited tonight, she told herself, because this was the first time she'd ever invited anyone over on her own.

But no one quite like Alex, she acknowledged. She'd never been able to talk to anyone the way she could talk to Alex Farmer.

This meal was merely reimbursement, if you like, for Alex's forbearance, her supportive observations. Alex was so down-to-earth that Jo had had the first glimmer of hope that she just might be able to get her disastrous life into some perspective.

And she was really looking forward to seeing Alex again. She'd invited her to dinner last week, when Alex had taken the photographs, and Jo hadn't seen her since she'd dropped Alex at the garage to collect her repaired motorcycle.

Most of that time Jo had spent painting, but on the couple of occasions she'd ventured down to the village she'd found herself unconsciously listening for the sound of a motorcycle or looking for Alex's tall figure.

Now Jo glanced at her wristwatch. Almost time. Nervousness clutched at her stomach again, and she bit her lip. Had she put on the outside light? She was halfway across the room when the doorbell rang loudly, echoing in the small room, and Jo jumped. She'd definitely forgotten to warn Alex that you could hear that doorbell for miles.

Jo reached the door, took a steadying breath, and turned the knob.

CHAPTER SEVEN

"Quite a fanfare." Alex indicated the doorbell. "Is it also designed to frighten unwelcome guests?"

Jo laughed breathlessly. "Sort of resounds, doesn't it? I think the previous tenant must have been hard of hearing." Her eyes slid over the other woman and away again, embarrassedly aware that she mustn't allow Alex to see her scrutiny. But it was proving difficult for Jo to drag her eyes from her.

Alex wore a cream cheesecloth dress, cut in panels joined by strips of matching crocheted lace. Crocheted straps left her tanned shoulders bare, the bodice molding her full breasts. A gold chain belt encircled Alex's waist, accentuating the curve of her rounded hips.

Once again Jo felt a rush of feeling, a mixture of admiration, of envy. And something else she barely recognized, but it made her mouth go dry and her heartbeats begin to thunder in her ears. Jo knew instinctively that in any gathering Alex would be the cynosure of male eyes.

Alex raised her dark eyebrows questioningly, and Jo apologized again. "I'm sorry. Your dress looks wonderful," she finished awkwardly. "Did you come by taxi?"

Alex shook her head. "No. On the bike. No mean feat," she added, at Jo's surprised expression. "Wearing dresses on motorcycles is a true art, which I can modestly say I've mastered. And I do do it modestly. With the help of my leather jacket and an old pair of jeans."

Jo chuckled. "I'm overcome with admiration." She stood aside. "Come in. And welcome to my mansion."

Alex stepped inside and glanced around the one-room apartment. "At least it won't take hours to vacuum," she said. "Vacuuming is my least favorite domestic chore."

"Then you'd love this place. It comes restricted to brooms." Jo glanced at the lighted window of the Cravens' living room and wondered if Mrs. Craven had heard the clanging doorbell and looked out to see who her visitor was. Quickly she closed the door for privacy. "Please. Sit down. Choice of couch or only chair."

But Alex had crossed to the bookcase and picked up the framed pencil sketch Jo had set there. "One of yours?" she asked.

"Yes. From years ago."

It was of a couple of oystercatchers stalking the water's edge in search of food. She'd caught the birds with their feet in the ebbing waves, their reflections hazily depicted in the wet, surf-covered sand.

Jo wondered why she kept it, how she could look at it without being reminded of that awful time. She'd sketched it on her honeymoon while Ben was off playing squash. Her honeymoon. What a misnomer.

Looking back as objectively as she could, Jo could scarcely believe she could have been so innocent of the minimum of basic sexual facts. Did every woman feel so bad the first time, she had often wondered, but she'd never had the nerve to put the question to anyone.

Her mother, well into middle age by the time Jo was married, would have been so embarrassed if Jo had broached the subject with her. And she'd had no really close girlfriends, not ones she could ask such intimate questions.

The pain on her wedding night had been awful, made her cry out, but Ben had continued to thrust into her. He'd been full of apologies afterward, but Jo had lain awake for hours after his steady breathing indicated he slept. Even now memories of her honeymoon still had the quality of a nightmare.

"It's fantastic." Alex continued to look at the sketch, and Jo pulled her thoughts back to the far more pleasant present.

"Thanks. I always liked it." And strangely it had been the only one she'd packed when she left.

Alex set the drawing back on the bookcase at last and crossed to the couch, glancing back at the sketch before sitting down. "Would you like some wine before the meal?" Jo asked easily. "Or I've got some scotch and ginger ale or soda water?"

"I'd love a small glass of wine. Are you having some?"

"I don't usually." Jo set the vegetables cooking and, taking the bottle of wine from the cooler, she twisted the opener. The cork came out with a pop. "However, tonight I think I will."

"Living dangerously, are we?" Alex quipped as Jo handed her a glass of wine and sat in the chair opposite her.

"Living dangerously? What's that? I don't know if I'd recognize it if it sat up and bit me," Jo laughed ruefully.

"You can always make a momentous change." Alex sipped her wine, her dark eyes holding Jo's.

Jo looked away. "I told you I was totally boring. I've always taken the safe road. Less problems that way."

"Most of us do that for most of our lives. But a selective moment of weakness can be very exhilarating."

"It can?" Jo rolled her eyes. "I think I'll continue on my safe road just for the moment. I fancy I'm too fragile for anything else."

"Pity." Alex twisted her wineglass in her fingers. "I was going to suggest a spin on the bike for appetizers."

Jo glanced across at her in alarm. Then she saw the twinkle in Alex's eyes and laughed. "For one terrifying moment you had me there," she said and stood up to check the vegetables.

Alex crossed over to the bookcase again. She glanced through the few books Jo had placed on the top shelf.

Most of Jo's books were still stored in the spare room of the house where Ben and Janet were now living, waiting with her other things to be collected. Jo hadn't had the courage to face that chore yet, but she knew she would have to do so soon.

"You like poetry?" Alex was turning the pages of one of the books.

"Yes." Jo stirred the casserole and put the lid back in place. "My taste's fairly erratic, but I do like romantic stuff."

"I haven't read any of Rod McKuen's in years," Alex said absently. "Brings back memories."

"My brother always liked his, and he started me reading it. I even fancied myself as a poet when I was at school. Won a couple of prizes in literary competitions." Jo laughed derisively. "I think I liked the tragedy of it all."

"Did you keep any of your work?"

Jo shrugged. "I think they're packed away at my parents' house. I doubt I'd be game to get them out and read them now. Wouldn't want to lose my illusions if they turned out to be dreadful."

"It's amazing how poetry stays with you, isn't it?" Alex picked up another book. "I couldn't remember a math equation if my life depended on it, but I frequently recall snatches of the poetry I did at school." Her lips twisted as she gave a soft, self-deprecating laugh. "When I feel I'm getting too big for my boots a little voice inside me recites off that poem by Shelley about Ozymandias, King of Kings, and his downfall."

"'I met a traveler from an antique land,'" Jo quoted.

Alex nodded. "That's the one. Keeps me humble." Alex replaced the book on the shelf.

"You don't strike me as the big-headed type," Jo remarked as Alex walked over to see what Jo was doing.

"Even Homer sometimes nods," she said dryly.

"Let's cross our fingers and toes that I haven't tonight when it comes to my cooking skills," Jo said with feeling. "I hope you like apricot chicken, my version of the recipe, with vegetables and garlic bread."

"If it's as delicious as it smells, I'm going to love it. Can I help serve or is everything under control?"

"The latter, I hope." Jo took the vegetables out of the microwave and began to set them on the warmed plates. "You can top off the wineglasses if you like."

"That I can handle."

They sat chatting over the meal, which Jo decided with relief was one of her better efforts. Later she brewed some coffee and they moved into the living area.

Alex was now sitting in the lounge chair, and Jo

sipped her coffee and relaxed on the couch. The couple of glasses of wine she'd had with the meal made her feel decidedly mellow.

"Want a refill?" She started to get up, but Alex waved her back into her seat.

"I'll get it." She stood and walked over to the workbench. "How about you?"

"No, thanks. This will be fine. Too much coffee at night and I end up spending the night with my eyes as wide open as saucers."

Alex crossed to the door and looked out into the darkness at the rain that had started to fall while they were eating dinner. "I think the rain seems to be easing a little. Isn't it typical. These showers were forecast for later in the week."

She came back, and this time she sat down on the couch beside Jo. There were a good two feet between them, but suddenly Jo felt warm and her skin tingled. As though Alex was sitting against her. She took a hurried sip of her coffee and almost choked.

Alex reached over and took her cup while Jo spluttered into her napkin.

"Sorry." She took the cup back from Alex, careful not to let their fingers touch. "That went down the wrong way."

"Okay now?" Alex asked with concern, and Jo nodded.

"So what other movies have you seen lately?" Jo asked hurriedly. They had been discussing a movie they'd recently both enjoyed, and Jo clutched at the safety of the subject, while part of her wondered why she felt she needed the protection of conventional conversation.

Alex casually slipped off her shoes and tucked her legs up under her, resting back against the arm of the couch so she was facing Jo. She mentioned a movie and Jo made some comments. Yet all the while Jo was aware of Alex sitting so close beside her. Only a small part of her mind was on the conversation. Mostly her mind was trying to formulate questions she couldn't quite grasp. Or didn't want to grasp.

"Well, it's getting late and you look tired," Alex said, glancing at the large gold watch on her tanned wrist. "I should be making a move."

Jo blinked. "But it's raining much more heavily now. You'll get wet. And I've heard some thunder as well."

"I've got my jacket on the bike, so half of me will be dry." She made a face as she stood up. "I meant to put my wet-weather gear in the panniers, but I forgot." A flash of lightning lit the darkness outside the windows, and a loud clap of thunder shook the crockery on the sink. "On second thought, perhaps I'll splurge on a taxi."

"I don't like your chances of getting a taxi at this time in this weather." Jo pushed herself to her feet. "You can stay the night if you like," she then heard herself say, and the warmth of a flush washed her cheeks. "If you don't mind sharing the bed." She indicated the couch.

Alex gave her a level look, but before she could reply another bright flash of lightning and a seemingly simultaneous clap of thunder broke overhead.

"Wow! That was close." Jo walked across to pull the curtains and shut out the lightning.

"You're probably right about the taxi. It will most

likely take hours." Alex looked at the time again. "But I feel bad about imposing myself on you."

Jo smiled. "You wouldn't be doing that. Believe me, you'd be doing me a favor. I hate storms. My father used to explain to me the practical how, when, where, and why of them, but knowing all that doesn't help." Jo shivered as another clap of thunder seemed to burst overhead.

"Perhaps that sort of anxiety stems from a storm that occurred in your childhood," Alex suggested as they both returned to the couch. They swapped anecdotes until the storm moved away, although the rain still came down in a torrent, beating a loud tattoo on the corrugated-iron roof.

"Think it's safe to have a shower now?" Jo asked.

Alex laughed. "I think so. I counted twenty miles on the last flash and roll."

"You take first turn." Jo stood up and went to the cupboard for a clean towel. "I've washed the T-shirt and shorts you loaned me. Do you think you could sleep in them?"

"They'll be fine."

Jo showed her to the small bathroom and hurried back to fill the sink with hot water for the dishes before Alex got into the shower. She left the washed dishes in the drainer and then crossed to her chest of drawers.

She usually slept in an old oversize T-shirt, but she dug in her drawer for a new nightshirt she'd bought some time ago. It was more circumspect, even if it did have a cute teddy bear and numerous red hearts all over the front.

Alex reappeared in her shorts and T-shirt, and after one quick glance at her Jo slipped into the shower herself. When she came out, a little self-conscious in her nightshirt, Alex had dried the dishes and stacked most of them away.

"You didn't have to do that," Jo said hurriedly.

Alex shrugged. "I hate waking to dishes in the sink in the morning, be they dirty or clean."

"I know what you mean. Thanks for doing them." Jo walked over to the couch and quickly folded it out before finding some extra pillows for Alex. "I'll just get some clean sheets."

"Don't worry about that. If you're anything like me you only sleep on one side of a double bed anyway."

"Yes, I do. I think I might resort to a single bed when I eventually get a flat in Brisbane. I'm sort of used to huddling on the edge because Ben always spread himself over most of the bed. So you won't have to worry about me pushing you off the other side."

"I'm relieved about that," Alex said.

Jo laughed. "What about you?" she asked as she crossed to switch out the overhead light, leaving the lamp beside the bed still burning, casting a warm glow.

"Oh, I keep pretty much to my own space most of the time."

"It's strange how when you're married you adjust to the other person and suddenly it's a habit. Take away the other person and you still keep to your habit."

"That'll pass, Jo. In no time you'll find yourself stretching out from corner to corner."

"But hopefully not tonight, I hear you say." Jo smiled, and Alex bent over to fold back her side of the bedclothes, her striking face in shadowy profile, her expression inscrutable.

And suddenly Jo sensed a tension in the air, as though the lightning had left a residue of charged particles behind that now began to clash heavily.

She watched Alex, just as unexpectedly wondering about Alex's bedmates, and she blushed at the intimacy of her thoughts. Alex looked up. Flustered by Alex's steady gaze, Jo said the first thing that came into her mind. "Have you ever been married, Alex?"

CHAPTER EIGHT

"Yes, I was married."

Jo raised her eyebrows in surprise. What she'd expected Alex to say she didn't know, but she recalled Mrs. Craven's ominously delivered confidence, She's not married, you know.

"I somehow didn't think you had been," Jo said as she sat down on the bed.

"Isn't everyone entitled to one mistake?" Alex had placed a couple of pillows behind her and rested back against them. "It was a long time ago." She grimaced. "Pushing twenty years, as a matter of fact. A lifetime, I guess."

"But you're not married now?"

"No," Alex replied emphatically.

"What happened?" Jo asked before she considered that the question might be unacceptable to the other woman. "I mean . . . I'm sorry, Alex. That was a pretty personal question. I didn't mean to intrude on your privacy."

Jo could feel contrite about that piece of blatant stretching of the truth. In reality she wanted to know everything about this fascinating woman.

"Don't worry if you don't want to talk about it," she added quickly, but Alex simply shrugged.

"As I said, it was a long time ago, and I admit I don't talk about it much. In fact it seems like it happened to someone else now.

"There wasn't anything out of the ordinary about it. I got myself into trouble." Her full lips twisted wryly. "Do they still use that awful euphemism for getting pregnant? Well, back then as you can imagine there was still a stigma attached to it, especially in a small country town.

"To add insult to injury, I was the daughter of the respected headmaster of the school, and his father was the local Uniting Church minister. Can you imagine the furor that caused?"

Jo shook her head. "World War Three?" she suggested lightly, and Alex laughed ruefully.

"Just about."

"So what did your respective parents say? I guess they were horrified."

"Horrified. Distraught. I doubt there are enough adjectives to describe our parents' reactions. But we

84

were in front of the altar at the said Uniting Church so fast our feet didn't have a chance to touch the ground. Our mothers pulled out all stops. I had a white dress and two bridesmaids, and Rick had a haircut and a borrowed suit."

"Wow!"

Alex laughed again. "It was an impressive effort, I can tell you. I can remember thinking after the ceremony, I've married a stranger, someone I don't even know, which wasn't quite the truth. We'd gone to school together for a couple of years, but we were still kids. I was just seventeen, and he was a so much older eighteen and a half."

Alex sighed, and Jo wanted to ask her about the child but somehow couldn't bring herself to. Her throat closed on a mixture of curiosity and foreboding.

She slid a quick glance at Alex. Alex was absently looking at a pattern on the cushion she held in her hands, but Jo knew she wasn't seeing it.

The silence stretched between them, and Jo swallowed nervously.

"My son was born six months later," Alex continued at last, her deep voice flat. "We wanted to call him Zack, but his grandmothers were appalled. He was christened Andrew James after his grandfathers, but I still secretly thought of him as Zack." Alex sighed again and looked across at Jo. "It was all pretty traumatic. I got up one morning when he was a couple of months old and he wasn't breathing. They call it sudden infant death syndrome now."

"Oh, no." Jo reached across and clasped Alex's arm. "It must have been dreadful for you. And for your husband."

85

"It was pretty awful. Things weren't the same after that, between Rick and me, that is. In retrospect I can see we both turned it all in on ourselves, but I couldn't seem to help myself at the time. It took me ages to stop blaming myself."

She gave a soft, mirthless laugh. "I thought it was divine retribution for my sins. I don't know what Rick thought. We were in the middle of renovating an old house his grandmother had left him, and after we did that and sold it we went our separate ways. He joined the army, eventually remarried, and at last count had six kids."

Jo didn't know what to say. She suddenly became aware she was gently rubbing the smooth skin of Alex's arm, and she drew her hand away. If Alex noticed she gave no indication.

"So. That's my sad story."

"I'm sorry," Jo said inadequately.

Alex nodded. "I would have made a rotten mother, so the poor kid was at least saved from that. I left our small town when Rick and I broke up," she continued quickly. "I came to Brisbane, got a job, and bought another old house. I mean, I was an experienced renovator by then." She smiled. "A couple of properties later I ended up here."

"And you never felt the urge to remarry?" Jo asked quietly, and Alex laughed out loud.

"Not really," she said with emphasis, and Jo laughed with her.

Alex slid down in the bed, and Jo slipped beneath the sheets, careful not to infringe on Alex's space. "Shall I put out the light?"

"Sure. Whenever you're ready," Alex murmured.

Jo flicked off the lamp, plunging them into an enveloping darkness. "Alex?"

"Mmm."

"Have you had many relationships?" Jo felt as though she didn't dare breathe as she waited for Alex to answer what she knew was an audacious question. Unless she chose not to answer. Jo swallowed quickly.

"Many? No. A few." She paused. "Let's just say I haven't been a saint, neither would I be classed as fast and loose." She shifted her position in the bed, and Jo tensed. "How about you?"

"Me?" Jo got out. "You mean, relationships?"

"Mmm."

"Oh. Well . . ." Jo stammered. "Ben was my first boyfriend and I was, well . . . I didn't . . . There was only Ben." She finished and wondered if Alex thought she was a prissy little Goody Two Shoes.

"You never felt attracted to anyone else and had to fight the urge to stray?"

"No, never," Jo replied honestly. "Does that make me sound passé?" she finished softly.

Alex sighed. "Not at all. It does make me wonder why Ben didn't realize he was on to a good thing."

It was Jo's turn to give a humorless laugh. "Oh, Ben would tell you I had my drawbacks. I wasn't exactly the life of the party, in or out of bed." Jo gulped, wondering what had possessed her to say something so personal, so embarrassing. And to Alex Farmer of all people. She cringed in mortification, wishing she could take back the words. Men would never find Alex wanting, even if Ben would have said she was overweight for his taste.

"It takes two to make a satisfying sexual relationship," Alex said evenly, and some of the tension eased in Jo.

"I've told myself that," Jo said without emotion, "but some of the time I don't believe myself. Perhaps I should have had an extramarital affair or two. Maybe that was my problem."

"And maybe you didn't have a problem," Alex countered. "Perhaps the problem was Ben's."

Jo sighed. "It's all relative now. I suppose apportioning the blame is a pointless exercise. But it certainly doesn't make me want to go searching for another relationship, that's for sure."

Alex was silent for long moments. "Who knows? When the right person comes along you might surprise yourself."

"You mean it'll be all right on the night?" Jo quipped.

Alex laughed softly. "Something like that." She settled in the bed. "Goodnight, Jo."

" 'Night, Alex," Jo replied. "And thanks."

"For what? I'd be wary of free psychoanalytical advice, if I were you."

"Makes a change from repetitive self-analysis."

Jo lay in bed listening to Alex's steady breathing. She fancied she could smell the faint aroma of her soap on Alex's body, and she wanted to lean closer, draw in the clean, fresh scent of her.

And she wanted to feel the warmth of her body. Not just Alex's body, she told herself. Anybody's body. She felt in need of the security, the safeness of another person's closeness.

Alex would be soft. And yet, Jo knew instinctively, she would exude her own quiet strength. She fought the longing to roll over, mold herself into the curve of Alex's back.

Jo grew suddenly hot and her muscles tensed, that same tingling dancing a crazy spiral in the pit of her stomach. She turned over, facing away from the other woman, and clung to the edge of her side of the bed. And it was a long time before sleep overcame her.

She felt warm, filled with well-being. Her naked skin made a soft, sensuous sound as she shifted on the satiny sheets.

She was sleepy, but her body felt vibrant, alive. It tingled where her fingertips touched . . .

Her nipples were aroused, and she closed her eyes as wild, erotic sensations surged from her breasts to the center between her thighs.

Her legs tensed, then parted, and she yearned for, craved the intoxicating release. But a small part of her knew that release would be denied her. It always was.

Yet still she sought that wonder, begged for the softness to cover her, to meld with her, to make her whole.

Jo moaned softly, rolled over, reached out and felt a sensation of someone else's body heat. She was drawn to the wonderful warmth, gently settled herself against it, and her entire body seemed to sigh.

A strong arm came around her, firm fingers splayed over her back, and she melted into the exhilaration of such closeness.

She inhaled an almost intoxicating perfume, a faint, heady scent of musk, and she thought she murmured someone's name. Yet she couldn't quite make out the syllables.

She stirred, seeking. Then someone reassured her with a soft, so soothing sound. Her agitated body relaxed as she slipped into a deep untroubled sleep.

Jo hovered in the peaceful realms between being asleep and awake. And she knew she'd been dreaming that dream again. Yet tonight it had been even more well-defined, more intense. Far more satisfying somehow. And yet still so elusive.

She shifted, still caught in her relaxed state, and her foot touched the warm flesh of another body. Ben. Were they late for work? Then reality surfaced. Ben was gone. In a flash she panicked as she came fully awake, before she realized the person beside her was Alex Farmer. And that Alex's tanned hand rested naturally on Jo's waist.

Tensed, Jo held herself as still as she could, not daring to move. Then she slowly slid away until Alex's hand released her and settled on the bed between them.

Alex was lying on her side, her face turned in Jo's direction, so close that Jo could see each individual eyelash fanned out on her cheek, see the faint color of freckles on the bridge of her nose. Feeling slightly guilty, as though she was invading Alex's privacy, Jo continued to watch her.

In repose Alex looked younger. The softened curve of her cheek and her full mouth added a vulnerability to the usually strong features.

Yet with that defenselessness there was still an air of strength, of safety, and Jo fought that same almost irresistible urge to move back across the small space between them and cuddle into Alex's warmth and security.

She wanted to burrow into Alex like a small child into its mother. And yet, not quite like that.

As Jo wrestled with her unsettling emotions Alex's dark eyes opened. She blinked once and then seemed to be immediately alert. Their eyes met, held, and Jo's stomach muscles clenched at the diversity of sensations that surged through her.

Quickly she pushed the unfamiliar, the alien feelings to the back of her mind. She'd examine them later, she told herself. If she dared.

And then she saw herself for one split second in her dream, naked, aroused, reaching out, before she blanked out the image she saw of Alex moving over her, onto her.

Jo felt as though all her breath had left her. She was burning hot, her skin aflame, and she wanted to flee, to escape her lustful thoughts.

She had to calm herself, and she drew a steadying breath. "What would you like for breakfast?" she asked quickly, and Alex stretched before replying.

"So you give all your bedmates breakfast, do you?" Alex asked teasingly, and Jo's guilty flush deepened.

"Only those who don't snore," she replied with a forced laugh.

Alex raised her eyebrows. "I think I'm safe. I've never had any complaints about that." She sat up, straightening her T-shirt over her full breasts, and Jo made herself look away.

"I usually just have toast or cereal, but I can do you some eggs if you'd like."

"Toast will be fine. And then I'd better head off. I want to make a start on the frames for the photographic competition."

Jo climbed out of bed and checked the water level in the electric kettle before switching it on. "I'm going to go and see the exhibition of the competition entries on Saturday. It was advertised in the local paper. Should be interesting. Especially yours," she added as she glanced over her shoulder at Alex.

"I was going to check out the exhibition myself," Alex continued. "Want to come with me on the bike?"

Jo fumbled with the slices of bread she was putting in the toaster and Alex laughed.

"Don't tell me you aren't game?" she mocked Jo lightly.

Jo swallowed. "Of course I'm game." The desire and aversion to being so close to Alex warred inside her, merged with what she considered her less than adventurous nature. Unconsciously, she straightened her backbone. "I'll try anything once," she quipped valiantly.

"Anything?" Alex asked softly, and Jo moved to open the refrigerator door to disguise the shiver that washed over her.

"Well, almost anything," she said as lightly as she could. "Jam or honey?"

"Decisions! Decisions!" Alex gave a feigned frown. "I'll try honey," she said with a grin as she walked across the room to switch off the whistling kettle.

"When will you know if you've won a prize?" Jo asked, seeking safe conversational ground as they chatted relatively easily over breakfast.

"When I appear at the show on Saturday I

suppose. Unless they have a policy of calling successful entrants. So. What time shall I pick you up? One o'clock?"

Jo nodded. "Sounds fine. But if it's raining we'll take my car. Okay?"

Alex pretended to give the option careful consideration. "That's a fair deal." She grinned. "You sugar baby, you."

Jo laughed regretfully.

"Let's say, the bike in full sunshine, the car if it even looks remotely like rain." Alex relented.

"Okay. I'm really looking forward to it," Jo said, wondering what Alex Farmer would think if she qualified that statement. Wondered how she could qualify that statement to herself.

Alex pushed back her chair. "Let's do the dishes, and then I'll be off."

"I think I can manage two plates and two mugs. Not that I'm wanting to get rid of you," Jo added hastily.

Alex laughed. "I was going to say I wouldn't want to outstay my welcome, but after coming for dinner and staying for breakfast that seems a little inappropriate," she said dryly. She opened the door and turned back to Jo. "But thanks, Jo. For dinner and the bed. And the breakfast."

"My pleasure." Jo smiled. "At least it's not raining this morning."

Alex glanced at the sky. "No, but I don't think the rain's gone. It's still pretty humid."

She took her leather jacket from the pannier on her bike, replaced it with her folded up dress, and then shrugged into her jacket. Deftly she kicked the stand back and began wheeling the bike from under the carport along the driveway toward the gate. Jo followed, regretful now that Alex was leaving.

Alex's gaze met Jo's briefly before she swung her long leg over the bike and settled on the seat. "See you Saturday then," she said lightly as she switched on the ignition. The engine roared, and with a wave Alex headed off down the road.

Jo stood watching her until she'd disappeared around the bend before she turned back to the house. She shivered at the thought of climbing on the back of the motorcycle, but with surprise she realized her feelings were more anticipation than alarm. And she resolutely pushed thoughts of her dream to the back of her mind.

"Morning, Jo." Mrs. Craven opened her door and met Jo on the driveway.

"Oh. Hello there, Mrs. Craven. That was a pretty wild storm we had last night, wasn't it?"

"Yes. I was going to pop in to see if you were all right, but I knew you had a visitor." The old woman looked expectantly at Jo.

"I can't say I like storms but," Jo shrugged, "I was fine. There was no need for you to worry."

"Now, dearie, of course I worry about you. So does Dad. 'You'd better go and check on Joanna and her visitor, Mother,' Dad said to me, but I didn't want to intrude."

Jo sighed. "Alex Farmer, the woman who took those lovely photographs on the cards I bought at the craft shop, she came over. She let me onto her property to do some sketching, so I thought I'd ask her to dinner as a sort of thank you." Jo shifted from one foot to the other as Mrs. Craven's weathered brow furrowed.

"Alex Farmer? The woman who rides that big motorcycle?" Molly Craven pursed her lips. "I'm sure it was very kind of her to let you do your sketching, Jo. But don't you think she's a bit of a strange one?"

"She's very nice," Jo began lamely, and Mrs. Craven's frown deepened.

"Gwen Price down the road was saying she thought Alex Farmer lived on a commune near Maleny," she said, and Jo raised her eyebrows in surprise.

"Oh, no. She has a lovely house with a remarkable view of the mountains."

"Does she now? And does she live on her own then?" Molly Craven's eyes sharpened behind her spectacles.

"As far as I know." Jo moved a few paces toward her open door, but the old woman followed her.

"I *had* heard she wasn't married. I told Gwen Price that." She regarded Jo inquiringly, but Jo made no comment. "She looks very mannish, wearing those pants and that black jacket and riding that motorcycle."

Jo reached her doorway and had to prevent herself from breathing a sigh of relief. "Well, I should get back to my painting," Jo said quickly. "I want to finish the scene I'm working on. Will you excuse me, Mrs. Craven?"

Jo escaped inside and closed the door firmly before the other woman could object. She heard her move away and then the door to the main house close.

She washed their breakfast dishes and tidied the flat before setting out her painting paraphernalia.

With great determination she refused to dwell on Mrs. Craven's observations or her own forbidden thoughts, and soon she was engrossed in her work.

"Now, all you have to do is put your foot on here and throw your leg over the seat," Alex said, grinning across at Jo.

"Right. Just throw my leg over the seat," Jo repeated dryly. "Somehow I didn't have the correct perspective in my mind. I don't remember the bike being this high. If I had I'd have gone into training for the big day."

"This is not a large bike, Jo," Alex told her.

Jo shot her a skeptical look. Since she'd last seen Alex, Jo had convinced herself she'd imagined her ridiculous fancies. There'd been no more dreams, and she now had her relationship with Alex back into perspective.

She pulled at the leg of her jeans and lunged, and to her surprise she ended up on the seat behind Alex. She wriggled experimentally and found the seat reasonably comfortable. But she didn't know quite where to put her hands.

Around Alex, she told herself with pseudocalm logic, suspecting she'd never be able to balance on the back of the moving machine without hanging onto something.

"There. That wasn't so bad, was it?" Alex looked over her shoulder at Jo as Jo moved the helmet Alex had given her into a firmer position on her head. "You climbed on like a professional. Are you sure you haven't been on a bike before?"

"Oh, no," Jo said honestly.

"Haven't been secretly moonlighting on the circuits, have you?"

"Of course not," Jo denied quickly, and then realized Alex was teasing her. She grinned reluctantly. "If I looked professional, it was just beginner's luck. And I might add I don't feel very safe. I feel as if I'm standing too near the edge of an extremely high cliff."

"First-time jitters." Alex stated. "Just put your arms around me and hang on."

Jo tensed. Her hands were resting on her jean-clad thighs but for some reason she couldn't quite bring herself to do as Alex bid her.

CHAPTER NINE

Just put your arms around me, Alex had said. Jo's stomach muscles twisted at the thought, and she told herself she was simply nervous about the coming ride. She had a sudden flash of her body molding itself to Alex's broad back, her arms sliding in slow motion until they encircled Alex's warm flesh. Jo gulped as her stomach twisted again, this time the sensations spiraling way lower.

At that disturbing moment Alex kicked the starter

and the bike gave a throaty roar, the seat beneath Jo immediately vibrating. Without further consideration, Jo's arms encircled Alex's body in instant panic.

"One small problem." Alex turned again as she throttled back the roar of the engine. "It might be a good idea if I get to breathe."

Jo swallowed. "Oh, I'm sorry. I didn't mean to . . ." She made herself relax a little, and Alex chuckled as she put on her own helmet.

She paused and looked back at Jo. "I won't take any risks," she said seriously. "I don't at any time." She put on her helmet and slipped the engine into gear.

For the first couple of minutes Jo kept her eyes tightly closed. Then she opened them a slit. She felt the wind tug at the sleeves of her denim jacket, heard it whooshing past her helmet, and before she realized it she had relaxed and was actually enjoying the experience. She kept a firm hold on Alex, her hands clasped together across Alex's midriff, just below the swell of her breasts.

Jo's heartbeats accelerated, and she started to let go. At that moment the road took a sweeping curve and she tightened her hold again.

This was accepted behavior for passengers on motorcycles, she told herself forcefully. But she couldn't prevent a small part of her being absolutely aware of each nuance of change in Alex's body. She imagined she felt each breath Alex took, each movement of the strong muscles in her shoulders, her back, as the bike ate up the miles to the coast.

An eternity later Alex pulled the bike smoothly to

a halt and Jo climbed off. She stretched as unobtrusively as she could and slowly removed her helmet.

"So?" Alex looked at her with raised eyebrows. "How was it?"

"Umm. Fine. Very, umm, invigorating." Jo infused her voice with some enthusiasm, and Alex laughed out loud, causing a few nearby heads to turn in their direction.

"Now, now. Your biggest enemy is overacting." Alex chuckled. "But I'll give you another chance. You can ride back with me."

Jo made a face and handed Alex her helmet. She glanced around at the large collection of stalls displaying a range of various paraphernalia. Colorful scarves and wide-brimmed hats. T-shirts and batik skirts. Dried flowers and herbs. Pottery and crystals. And crowds of milling people.

"Popular place," she said.

Alex agreed. "They hold it every year, and every year it seems to get bigger. The painting and photography exhibits are over in the hall."

"Great," Jo said with enthusiasm. "Let's go."

The afternoon went quickly, and although the journey home on the back of the bike wasn't quite as frightening Jo rather doubted she was cut out for this type of travel. Alex turned into the open driveway and pulled up behind Jo's car.

She switched off the throbbing engine, and they climbed off.

"Home safely," she said as they both took off their helmets. "Was it too hair-raising?"

Jo shook her head. "No, not really. But I don't think I'll apply for membership with Hell's Angels just yet."

Alex laughed as she took Jo's purchases from the panniers and handed them to her. "There's your stuff. And one framed copy of your photo. I thought you might like to have one."

Jo took the parcels and the portrait. "Oh, Alex. Thanks for this. I really love it. And congratulations again on your success. Two prizes and a Highly Commended out of three entries. Not bad."

Jo looked at the photo Alex had printed for her, and she was again filled with amazement.

Alex had placed a wide-brimmed straw hat on the back of Jo's head. Jo's gray eyes sparkled clearly, and there was the faint dusting of light freckles across the bridge of her nose.

With clever lighting the pattern from the straw hat dappled her cheek. Jo's lips turned up in a small smile, the shadow of a dimple at the corner of her mouth.

"I still can't believe it. You make me look," Jo paused, "well . . ."

"Beautiful," Alex finished.

Jo blushed. "I wouldn't go quite that far," she said quickly. "But you seem to have caught my best side."

Alex laughed. "Remember, the camera never lies."

"Well, in this case, it's bent the truth considerably." Jo grinned. "And thanks for taking me with you to the craft show, too."

"Even if you did have to do a death-defying act

on this monster, hmm?" Alex leaned casually against the bike, one booted foot crossed over the other. "I've really enjoyed today, Jo. Maybe we —"

"Is that you, Jo?" Molly Craven opened her side door and came down the steps, eyeing Alex levelly.

"Oh. Hello, Mrs. Craven," Jo replied quickly. "Have you met Alex Farmer?" Jo made the introductions.

Alex put her helmet on the bike seat and held out her hand. "Nice to meet you."

Much to Jo's embarrassment, Molly Craven made no bones about sizing up the other woman. Her gaze ran over Alex's jeans and leather jacket before good manners obviously overcame her reticence and she held out her hand to Alex.

"We're just back from the craft show at Buderim," Jo told the older woman. "I know how much you like jam, so I bought you some of your favorite. Rosella." Jo held out the bottle, and Mrs. Craven took it from her.

"That's very thoughtful of you, dear. Thank you." She looked pointedly at Alex, who was clipping the spare helmet onto the back of the bike. "I'm not sure your mother would care for you riding about on one of those dangerous contraptions, Jo."

Alex swung her long leg over the motorcycle, but before Jo could defend her a tall, fair-haired man came down the steps and put his arm around the old woman's shoulders. Molly Craven turned to him with an adoring look.

"Oh, there you are, love. This is the someone I wanted you to meet." She indicated Jo.

"I'm Mike Craven, a prodigal grandson," the man said, his dancing green eyes settling on Jo's surprised face.

Alex moved, and the seat of the bike creaked, making the three pairs of eyes turn toward her. "Well, I'd best be off," she said as she reached for her helmet.

"Oh, I'm sorry." Jo touched Alex's leather-clad arm. "This is Alex Farmer, a friend of mine."

Mike's gaze ran over Alex and the motorcycle.

"Nice to meet you, Mike," Alex said casually before turning to Jo. "Thanks for coming to the show with me. I'll see you then." She glanced quickly at Mike Craven before she put on her helmet and turned the bike around, not starting the engine until she had cleared the driveway. The bike gave a throaty roar, and she headed off up the road.

Mrs. Craven tsked. "Noisy things those. And very unfeminine," she added with a frown.

Mike caught Jo's eye and grinned.

"Anyway," Molly Craven continued, "that's by the by. Come in for a cup of tea, Jo. I've just boiled the kettle, and I won't take no for an answer."

"Jo may not want a cuppa, Gran," Mike said easily, shrugging apologetically at Jo.

"A cup of tea would be nice," Jo capitulated, suppressing a sigh as she put her few purchases and the photo on the trunk of her car. Slipping off her denim jacket, she draped it over her parcels to collect on her way back.

"Wonderful. And this rosella jam will go so well with the scones I've just made. So nice of you to think of me, Jo." Mrs. Craven led them up into the cluttered but homey living room. "Come in and sit down."

Mike Craven waited until Jo was seated before lowering himself into one of the old-fashioned lounge chairs opposite hers.

"So you're renting Gran's flat," Mike began. "Are you on holiday?"

"Yes." Jo was a little self-conscious now that they were alone together.

"I am, too. I was off to Canada skiing with a friend, but he broke his leg so we called the trip off. I thought I'd take the opportunity to catch up with my grandparents, as well as visit some of my boyhood haunts." He made a face. "Don't they say a yen to take a nostalgic journey into the past is a sure sign of advancing age?"

Jo laughed and relaxed a little. "Perhaps it is. That doesn't mean you have to admit to it."

"Right." He sat back in the chair and thrust out his long legs. "Gran tells me you're divorced."

"Just about," she told Mike carefully.

He nodded. "I'm already divorced. Last year. Pretty traumatic, isn't it?"

"Yes, I guess it is."

They both fell silent for long moments, and then Mike sighed.

"Any kids?" he asked, and Jo shook her head. "I've got two. A boy seven and a girl six. We've tried to keep it as painless as possible for them but," he shrugged, "we had to decide whether two unhappy parents in the house together was worse than two a little less unhappy parents apart."

"I'm sorry. I can imagine it must have been awful."

"Yes. But the kids seem to be coping. Me, too, now." He shifted in his chair as his grandmother bustled in carrying a tray.

Mike quickly stood up to take it from her. "You shouldn't be carrying that, Gran. Why didn't you call me?" He set the tray down on the coffee table, and his grandmother patted his cheek.

"I didn't want to interrupt you and Jo having such a nice chat." She turned to Jo. "Why don't you pour the tea, love, while I fetch the scones."

Jo's heart sank as the older woman beamed from one to the other before she left them alone again.

"What are you doing tonight?" Mike's voice broke in on Jo's thoughts, and she glanced up at him in surprise. "Was that too blatant? I'm sort of out of practice. But I just thought you might like to go out for dinner."

"Oh. Well." Jo set the teapot down gently. "I don't know that I'd be such good company."

"No strings, Jo," Mike said seriously. "I'll be honest with you. I'm not in any hurry to get involved just yet, and you probably aren't either. But it would be nice to sit down over an enjoyable meal and just relax. What do you say? I'd appreciate the company."

"I suppose it would be all right," Jo agreed reluctantly.

"And it would get Gran out of matchmaking mode for a while." He laughed. "She doesn't think a man can manage on his own. She even tut-tutted over the way I'd ironed my shirts." He lowered his voice. "I didn't dare tell her they were drip-dry and that I hadn't ironed them at all."

Jo laughed with him, and Mrs. Craven positively glowed as she rejoined them.

"There now, don't you two seem to be getting on well."

Mike wagged his finger at his grandmother. "None of that, Gran. Otherwise Jo might change her mind about going out to dinner with me tonight."

"You're going out for dinner? Well, isn't that lovely."

Alone in her flat some time later, Jo wasn't so sure it was. She set the photo Alex had taken of her on top of her bookcase and admired it again. What she really wanted to do was sit down and think over her day at the craft show with Alex.

She turned and paced the floor, telling herself it was just a dinner date with Mike, nothing serious. He had said as much himself. Still, she hoped she hadn't done the wrong thing. Divorce made people vulnerable.

But at least she knew she wasn't interested in another relationship right now, she told herself. If she ever would be.

However, she'd committed herself to going out with Mike now, so she supposed she'd better have a quick shower and try to decide what she was going to wear. She had just kicked off her shoes when the phone rang.

"Hi!" Alex's deep voice brought an instant smile to Jo's face.

"Hi yourself! You must have made it home all right then?" Jo quipped.

Alex laughed. "You can ask that when I demonstrated my careful riding skills? Another deep wound to my poor ego."

"Just joking." Jo sat down and relaxed back into the chair, glancing again at the photo on the bookcase. "Tell your ego I was most impressed and I thoroughly enjoyed the day."

"I did, too." Alex paused for a moment. "I was thinking of inviting a couple of friends around after dinner tonight, and I thought if you're not too tired after your grand adventure on the bike you might like to come along as well."

Jo gave a soft, rueful laugh. "Well, I did have a big night planned watching TV, but as of an hour ago I've got a date, would you believe?"

The phone echoed hollowly for a long second. "Ah. Let me guess. Tall, blond, and nice looking?"

Jo laughed. "Yes to all three."

"He's a fast worker."

"He seems nice enough. He was divorced last year." Jo sighed. "I have a feeling he's still getting over it. And I also suspect it could be a long night."

"Do you think he needs a shoulder to cry on?"

"Maybe something like that. If he does it will be a case of the blind leading the blind." Jo pictured Alex standing by her breakfast bar. "I don't mean to sound awful, but in retrospect I think I'd rather be coming over to your place."

Alex laughed softly. "Is it too late to change your mind?"

"Afraid so. But thanks for the invitation, Alex," Jo said sincerely.

"I was just going to break open a bottle of bubbly to toast my successes, so do you want to make it next Saturday night instead? I haven't rung my friends yet and, come to think of it, it would give them a little more notice, too."

"That would be great. Are you sure you want to put it off till next week?"

"Probably more sensible anyway. I have to go down to Brisbane tomorrow. I've got some business to do down there, and I'll be away most of the week. What say we make it for dinner, six-thirty next Saturday?"

"Sounds great. Formal or casual, and what can I bring?"

"Definitely casual," Alex assured her. "And just bring yourself."

"Great. It will be something to look forward to."

"Okay. Well, I'll see you then."

"Have a good time in Brisbane," Jo said.

Alex gave a soft laugh. "With my accountant? Oh, sure." She paused.

"Oh, and Jo. You have a nice time tonight with tall, blond, and good looking."

It was Jo's turn to laugh. "I can but try."

CHAPTER TEN

Jo drove happily toward Maleny, the visor pulled down against the glare of the slowly sinking sun. She was humming softly to herself in anticipation of seeing Alex again.

The week had seemed a month long. And what a week it had been, she reflected, making a face at the winding road. She could almost laugh at the fact that this last week had been more eventful than the past year. Well, almost.

Her dinner with Mike Craven had turned out to be much less painful than she had expected it would be. They had driven along to a well-known restaurant in Montville, and Jo had found making conversation with Mike far less harrowing than she usually found such social occasions. Then again, Mike enjoyed talking, and it had been somewhat refreshing to realize he didn't always make himself the subject of his conversation.

She had even found herself wondering why his wife had chosen to divorce him. Still, she supposed you did have to live with someone to really know them. She'd learned that firsthand. Ben had always presented such a charming persona to the outside world.

Because of Mike's easy camaraderie, Jo had accepted his invitation to drive up to Noosa the next day. And on Tuesday they'd gone down into Caloundra to see a movie.

Enjoyable as his company was, however, Jo had been pleased that he had been committed to returning to Brisbane for the remainder of the week as he'd promised to visit his parents and his children.

The next few days Jo eagerly spent on her painting, and when the doorbell clanged yesterday afternoon her thoughts had immediately flashed to Alex. But Alex was in Brisbane, and Jo had surmised she wasn't due back until Saturday. As was Mike Craven. Maybe it was his grandmother.

She'd crossed to the door and glanced out through the glass panel. The sight of the tall figure standing frowning on the step had made her pause in surprise. Ben was the last person she'd expected to see.

Moving irritatedly he rapped on the wooden panel. Jo reached out and opened the door.

She stood gazing up at him, part of her trying to assess her emotions. He was still quite good looking, she supposed, in a dark and sulky sort of way. And she again wondered why, when she first met him, she hadn't recognized the petulant curve to his mouth, the hint of condescension in the lift of his head.

"Hello, Ben," she said evenly. "This is a surprise."

"Yes, I guess it is." He smiled at her. The same smile she'd thought so attractive now seemed somewhat artificial. "But not too bad a surprise, I hope." He looked past her, into her flat. "I thought you were living in the house. The old biddy directed me around here."

"I suppose you'd better come in," Jo said reluctantly, standing back, and Ben stepped inside.

"I had to drive up to Noosa to see a client, so I thought I'd look in on you on my way back."

"I see."

"I also needed to talk to you about the house," Ben added, sitting down on the couch without being invited to, his eyes roving around the room.

Jo made herself relax just a little and sat down opposite him, moving back in the chair when she realized she was perched tensely on the edge of the seat. "What about the house?" she asked evenly.

"Well." Ben shrugged. "Janet's not comfortable living there. And I was thinking I might sell it, buy something on the other side of town."

"I thought you didn't care for the other side of town," Jo reminded him a little brusquely. She'd wanted to make their home on this side of Brisbane to be nearer her parents, but Ben had insisted on the south side of the city.

111

"Janet's mother lives in the western suburbs. She's a widow, and Janet wants to live nearer to her."

"Does she?" Jo kept her expression bland. So Janet wanted to live closer to her mother, too, she thought bitterly, and Ben was going to indulge her. Janet must really have something going for her, she reflected and then sighed. What did she care now anyway? It had nothing to do with her. "Whatever you decide," she told him, and Ben spread out a little more on the couch, one arm along the back, one ankle resting on his other knee.

"I thought you might want first refusal."

"What makes you think I'd want to buy the house?"

He shrugged again. "Well, it was our home. I thought it was only fair to ask you."

"What would I do with a big house?" Jo shook her head. "No, I don't want it, Ben. I think it's best that you sell it. I certainly don't want to live there."

As she'd told Alex, she'd never liked the house. It was too much of a showpiece, situated in an expensive area amid rows of similar showpieces. And it had been Ben's status symbol. It had never really felt like a home to her.

"I just thought I should ask you, show you the consideration of giving you the opportunity to buy it if you wanted it. It has good investment potential."

"Thank you. But no thanks."

A heavy silence fell between them, and Ben looked around the flat again.

"This is pretty small, isn't it? How long will you be staying here?"

"A few months. As you know I took my long service leave. I felt I needed some time away from, well," Jo paused, "away from everything."

"I feel a bit like that myself." Ben sat forward, his hands clasped together, elbows on his knees. "I wish I could move away from everything and everyone just like that."

Just like that? He made it seem as though she'd waked up one morning and, having no responsibilities, she'd just lightly decided to take off. How like Ben to trivialize anyone else's actions. "You could take a holiday yourself. You must have stacks of time owing to you," she said with as much detachment as she could.

"I have, but I'm snowed under at the moment." He ran a hand tiredly over his jaw. "Couldn't get away if my life depended on it."

"If it did you'd have to, wouldn't you say?" Jo remarked. "They'd find someone else to do your job."

Ben shook his head. "Too much trouble trying to teach someone." He smiled crookedly. "No one would want to do it."

Jo refused to allow his self-satisfied expression to provoke her, although she had to make a concentrated effort not to do so. She wondered how Janet felt about Ben's obsession with his job. "Janet keeps telling me I need a break." Ben stood up restlessly, crossing to the bookcase, and he picked up the framed photograph that Alex had taken of Jo. "This a recent shot?"

"Yes. A friend took it," Jo added cautiously, and Ben turned back to look at her, eyes narrowed.

"You're seeing someone?"

"No. Of course not. It was just a friend who's interested in photography. She took it for a competition she was entering."

"Oh. A woman," Ben dismissed the answer easily.

"It took second prize," Jo told him, needing for some reason to validate Alex's achievement.

But Ben had moved on to the painting of the Glasshouse Mountains she'd put in a frame as a gift for Alex. He peered at the signature. "Have you taken up painting again?"

"I'm amazed you even remember I used to do it," Jo couldn't prevent herself from saying tersely.

He replaced the painting and turned back to her again, one hand resting on the top of the bookcase, his other shoved into the pocket of his slacks. "Of course I remember," he said.

Jo regarded him levelly.

"I remember lots of things about you, Jo. About us. It wasn't so bad, was it?" he asked softly and straightened, strolling toward her.

Jo stood up, tensing inside.

"I mean, maybe things fell apart a bit toward the end, but in the beginning, when we were first married, I thought we had a pretty good thing going between us."

Jo blinked, scarcely believing she was hearing him say this. It was a far cry from his brutal comments when he'd told her he was going to divorce her.

"I've missed you, you know," he said softly, his eyes dropping to the curve of her breast beneath her thin top. He again turned on the lopsided, little-boy grin she had thought was so attractive when she first met him, before they were married.

"Have you?" she asked flatly.

His slow sigh was, to all outward appearances, filled with regret. "Yes. I have."

"I'm surprised you've had time, what with your job, your family responsibilities," Jo got out between her teeth.

A small frown furrowed Ben's brow. "I have been flat as a tack," he agreed, her sarcasm going completely over his head. His gaze held hers intensely. "But I have thought of you often, Jo. About the good times we had."

He reached out, ran his hand down her bare arm, and Jo stepped back as though she'd been stung. She put the chair between them and glared across at him.

"I'm sure Janet would hardly be impressed by that, Ben."

"She knows I'm a free agent."

"A free —you have a young child, Ben. What about him?"

"Oh, Jamie's a great little kid but —" he shrugged — "believe me, fatherhood isn't all it's cracked up to be. I mean, I don't find it all-consuming. Maybe when he gets a bit older, when he can talk properly. You know."

Jo shook her head, wanting to say so much, but she was far too angry.

"Well, it's not as though Janet and I are married yet." He smiled conspiratorially at her. "And I certainly don't tell her everything I do."

Jo drew herself up to her full height. "What are you proposing, Ben? An affair with your ex-wife?"

"Legally you're still my wife. Besides, Janet needn't know. I told her I might have to stay over in Noosa, return tomorrow."

"You want to stay the night here with me? I can't

believe you're serious." Jo gazed at him incredulously. "We could jeopardize our divorce petition."

"Who'd know?" Ben asked with a shrug.

"I would. I'd know," Jo told him firmly.

"It could be our little secret." Ben grinned engagingly, and Jo bit back the urge to tell him just what she thought of the idea of his little secret.

She took a steadying breath. "I don't recall you being all that satisfied with our sex life. Or is it a case of the grass being greener?" she finished scathingly.

"Come on, Jo. Our sex life wasn't that bad. We had some good times."

"You might have." A small part of Jo stood apart from her, amazed at her forthrightness. A year ago she knew she'd have been incapable of taking such a stand against Ben. "I can't say I ever remember the earth moving for me."

Ben lifted his chin, his eyes narrowing, then he relaxed a little. "I thought you might be over your bitterness by now," he said, and Jo's knuckles turned white where her fingers clutched at the back of the chair.

"Bitterness? Why wouldn't I be bitter? Good grief, Ben! Listen to yourself! We're practically divorced, a divorce you insisted on, and now you're suggesting we let bygones be bygones and have a roll in the hay for old time's sake."

"For the sake of the good times," he said and Jo shook her head.

"I suggest you go now, Ben. Before I say something I might regret later."

Ben watched her, eyes speculative. "You've changed, Jo. I wonder why?"

"Perhaps I've grown up at last. Or maybe I've taken off my rose-colored glasses where you're concerned."

"Or perhaps you're getting it from someone else," Ben suggested.

"It?" Jo repeated through clenched teeth.

"Sex. Have you found someone else to sleep with, Jo?"

"No, Ben. I haven't. Not that it's any of your business."

He smiled smugly. "I was only stirring you. I knew you wouldn't be."

Jo raised her eyebrows. "Oh?"

"Well, you always were such a prudish little thing. You sure held me at arm's length until we were safely married. Always so insistent on doing what was right. I mean, it would be committing adultery, wouldn't it? You having it off with someone else when you're still married to me."

"I don't consider myself to be still married to you, Ben. And as far as I'm concerned Janet's welcome to you."

Ben shook his head. "Look, Jo. I can understand you might be a little angry with me for, well, because of Janet. And the baby. But I do regret hurting you, believe me. I did love you." He sighed softly. "I guess part of me always will."

Jo looked at him, and her anger faded away. What was the point anyway? she asked herself. Ben would never change. He would always be the spoiled, manipulative little boy forever wanting what he couldn't have, wanting everything his way.

"If it's forgiveness you want, Ben, then all right. I forgive you. Now, I think you should be going home to your family," Jo said flatly.

"I meant it, Jo. About loving you." He walked closer, leaned on the chair with one hand, resting the other lightly on her shoulder. "And I do still find you attractive."

Jo moved, and his hand fell from her shoulder. "Thank you, Ben. I appreciate that," she said dryly. "And just let me know when you decide what you're going to do with the house."

She turned toward the door, but he'd moved closer again.

"Come on, Jo," he said cajolingly. "If there's no one else, you must be really looking for it. Why don't you and I have a little fun? We used to have lots."

His arms came around her, and before she could offer any resistance he'd pulled her roughly to him, his mouth crushing her lips against her teeth, the faint taste of stale alcohol on his breath.

Jo struggled, pushing her hands against his chest, fighting to turn her head from his brutal kiss. She struck out at him with her foot, and he grunted as her shoe connected with his shin. Jo took advantage of the loosening of his grip to put space between them.

"How dare you, Ben! Don't touch me! Don't touch me ever again!" she got out angrily, holding one hand out as if to ward him off.

Ben lifted his leg and rubbed at his shin. "For

God's sake, Jo. That was totally unnecessary, and it hurt."

"It was meant to." Jo reached out with a shaking hand and turned the doorknob, opening the door. "I want you to leave now, Ben. And anything else you want to say to me you can do so through my attorney."

Ben straightened his tie. "You know, if you want a bit of free advice, Jo, you'd better lighten up," he said caustically. "Men don't want to waste time having to melt a block of ice. They want red-hot women. You might remember that when you start looking for a man. If you ever find one."

"Don't lose any sleep over it, Ben. I think you've cured me." Jo stepped outside and turned, waiting for him to follow her.

He brushed past her just as Mike Craven came around the side of the house.

"Hi, Jo!" He smiled broadly. "How are you?"

Ben gave a harsh laugh. "So that's how the land lies." He strode around Mike. "I hope you've got lots of sensitive New Age–guy patience, mate, because you'll need it," he sneered as he disappeared up the drive.

Mike turned back to Jo, fair eyebrows raised. "What's the problem, Jo?"

"My ex-husband." Jo grimaced.

"Want me to go after him?" Mike asked with a frown, and Jo shook her head.

"Not nearly worth it," she said flatly.

"Something tells me it wasn't a congenial meeting."

"That's very perceptive of you."

"Are you okay?" he asked gently, and Jo took a deep breath.

"I'm fine." She infused some measure of cheerfulness into her voice. "You're back early."

Mike raised his eyes skyward. "Mum was talking to Gran on the phone last night, and I've been dispatched to take my grandparents to Brisbane for the night. Mum's cooking a big spread. The whole bit."

"That will be nice." Jo made conversation while inside she was shaking from her altercation with Ben.

"I'm bringing them back tomorrow. So would you like to go out somewhere tomorrow night?"

"I can't tomorrow night, Mike. I'm already doing something. Thanks all the same though."

For a moment Jo thought he was going to ask her for details, but he nodded his head and gave her a quick smile. "Call me if your ex comes back for a second bout," he said and went into the main house.

Jo gave a wry smile as she signaled for a right turn. It had surely been some week. Alex wouldn't believe her when she told her all about it. Her smile broadened, and she unconsciously pressed a little harder on the accelerator.

Then Jo's smile faltered. On top of all that, she'd had that dream again the night before Ben turned up. And once again the dream had somehow become confusingly synonymous with Alex.

Jo frowned. But why would she suddenly associate

the dream with Alex? Perhaps, she thought, the dream was simply a result of the stress of the past months. So why hadn't she had the dream when Ben had asked her for a divorce? she asked herself.

Then she was turning into Alex's driveway and she made herself put all thoughts of the dream out of her mind.

Alex met her at the door, smiling a welcome. "Hi! You look great. Nice dress."

Jo grinned, a surge of pleasure washing over her. "Oh, this old thing." She waved a careless hand. "I've had it for years."

It had taken her ages to decide what to wear, and she'd finally settled on a simple wine-red dress that left her shoulders bare. But she was inordinately pleased that Alex liked her outfit.

"The rich color suits you," Alex told her easily, and Jo wanted to compliment the other woman on her own tailored slacks and multicolored peasant blouse, but she felt suddenly shy. The vibrant colors also suited Alex's dark good looks, adding to her sultry sensuousness.

"I just tried to phone you at the flat," Alex was saying, "but you were on your way and I couldn't remember your car-phone number."

Jo's smile faded a little. "You mean there's some problem? Is tonight off?"

"Well, not entirely. Unless you want it to be."

"Oh, no, of course not. What's happened to your friends?"

"They just called to cancel. Nikki and Fran have a fifteen-month-old son, and he's come down with something. They didn't want to bring him in case it's contagious, and they didn't want to leave him in case he fretted for them." Alex grimaced and stood back so that Jo could enter.

Alex had set the table for four, and she crossed over and removed two of the placemats. "So it looks like it's just us then."

"I don't mind," Jo said, refusing to examine the fact that she was far more pleased than she had any right to be that things had turned out this way. "Unless you don't want to be bothered . . ."

"After I've slaved over a hot stove all afternoon? No way."

Jo giggled, and Alex looked at her with eyebrows raised. "I just had this picture of you with your apron on, all floury as you kneaded the dough. Like those old chauvinistic advertisements for domestic products they used to have. The wife with her coiffured hair happily vacuuming the new carpet."

Alex burst out laughing. "You must have a vivid imagination. That's not a picture of myself I can bring to mind. And, apart from that, let me warn you I'm always on the lookout for someone prepared to slave in the kitchen for me."

"What you mean is, you need a wife," Jo said with a smile.

CHAPTER ELEVEN

Alex's dark eyes met hers, and Jo felt a rush of heat sweep over her. The earth moved just slightly off its axis and spun dizzyingly for wild immeasurable seconds. And then Alex broke the contact and turned to slip the unused placemats into a drawer.

Jo clasped at her disintegrating composure, her mouth suddenly dry with the shock of that earth-shattering moment. What had triggered such unconscionable flights of fancy?

"A wife? Now can you see me being so politically incorrect? Although I will admit in theory it sounds good," Alex said lightly as she moved toward the kitchen. "Would you like a glass of wine while I'm putting the finishing touches to dinner?"

Jo pulled herself together as some of the tension abated. "That would be lovely. Oh, nearly forgot." She handed Alex the parcel she'd held behind her back. "Open this before you get the wine."

"What is it?" Alex smiled at the white package festooned with curls of colored ribbon. "It looks too nice to disturb."

She pulled the watercolor from the opened end of the parcel and gazed at it in surprised delight. "Jo, it's great. You've captured the colors wonderfully."

"Do you think so?" Jo walked around the breakfast bar and glanced over at the painting. "I was hoping you'd like it. It's a sort of thank-you-for-letting-me-trespass gift. And for the portrait you did for me."

"You didn't have to do that. But I love it." Alex turned and touched Jo's arm.

Jo's skin tingled, her nerve endings danced. A shiver of pleasure ran up her spine, and she shifted from one foot to the other in case Alex saw her involuntary movement.

"I know exactly where I'm going to put it." Alex crossed back into the living room and held it experimentally on the wall over the television set. "What do you think?"

"Looks great." Jo smiled happily. "The tones match the wall and everything."

"Exactly. And I'll be able to look at it from my favorite chair." Alex stood it carefully on top of the TV. "I'll hang it later."

She walked back toward Jo. "Thank you." She

leaned forward and kissed Jo lightly on the cheek. "Now, how about the wine?"

Jo was pleased that Alex was engrossed in taking the bottle of wine from the fridge, because Jo's hand went involuntarily to her cheek, to the place Alex had touched with her lips, and she flushed deeply. A flutter of butterfly wings teased in the pit of her stomach, but she made herself ignore the strange sensation.

She walked over to take the glass from Alex's hand.

"To your painting, to my photography, and to our successes." Alex raised her glass and clinked it on Jo's, and they laughingly sipped their wine.

"You'll never believe the week I've had," Jo began enthusiastically as they sat down to eat. "Talk about everything happening at once, and all unexpected."

"Sounds interesting. So I guess my first question is how was your date with tall, blond, and good-looking?" Alex asked lightly and Jo raised her eyes expressively toward the ceiling.

"Surprisingly it was quite enjoyable. He did need a shoulder to cry on, but Mike's such a nice guy he did it so inoffensively. Actually, it was three dates with tall, blond, and good-looking." she added with a laugh.

"Three? Didn't I already say he was a fast worker? Well, triple that." Alex seemed intent upon her glass of wine. The red liquid caught the light from the candle, and it glowed richly. "You must have been impressed to go out with him three times."

Jo frowned. "I think I might have been exaggerating when I called them dates. Apart from the dinner on Saturday night, we went for a drive on

Sunday and then to the movies in Caloundra on Tuesday."

"Oh, I think it would be safe to call them dates," Alex said.

"Well, they were quite pleasant anyway. At least he didn't make any moves on me, which was a relief," Jo said with feeling.

"Don't fancy him?"

Jo frowned slightly. "It's not that exactly. He's a nice enough guy, probably loads nicer than most, but I just don't want to wake up and find myself in the same position I was in before — and a Ben with a different face beside me."

Alex raised her eyebrows. "You could simply have an enjoyable fling," she suggested, and Jo shook her head.

"No, thanks. I'm off men. Remember?"

"I do seem to recall your saying something like that. Most sensible," Alex said with mock seriousness.

"At least for a while." Jo grinned crookedly. "Like ten years."

"Bit extreme maybe." Alex took another sip of her wine. "What else made the week so action-packed?"

Jo groaned. "Ben turned up."

"Oh." Alex shifted her food around on her plate. "And you didn't expect him?"

"Not in a million years. He said he'd decided they didn't want to live in the house, our house, and he came to ask me if I wanted to buy it."

"And are you interested?"

"Definitely not. To tell you the truth, I never liked it." Quick flashes of memories passed through

Jo's mind, and she sighed. "I always felt like it belonged to someone else."

They fell silent. Jo wanted to tell Alex about the rest but she hesitated, wondering if Alex would have handled the situation differently. But no, she told herself. She hadn't let Ben walk all over her. She'd confronted him, sent him away.

"Strange he would think you'd want to go back there anyway," Alex said quietly.

Jo nodded. "He wanted to spend the night with me," Jo exclaimed before she could hold the comment in. "Can you believe that?"

Alex's dark eyes held Jo's stormy gray ones, and she shook her head.

"He'd planned the whole thing, the bastard. He told Janet he might have to stay overnight in Noosa on business."

"That's convenient," Alex commented derisively.

"He said he remembered the great times we'd had, that he still cared about me and why shouldn't we enjoy a bit of sex for old time's sake." Jo shook her head. "When I reminded him of his responsibilities toward his family, he said fatherhood wasn't all it's cracked up to be. My God! The anguish he put me through pressuring me about having a child —" Jo stopped, realizing she was again revealing more to Alex than she had to anyone. She lifted her glass and drained the rest of her wine.

Alex reached across the table, took Jo's hand, and gave it a squeeze. "Bastard is right," she agreed gently.

"I reminded him of our far from perfect

relationship, and then he tried to kiss me. So I kicked him."

Alex chuckled. "Good for you. That would have cooled his ardor. Or should I say, lowered his mainsail?"

Jo bit off a giggle. "Unfortunately, the kick wasn't high enough. But he should have a lovely bruise on his shin," she added with relish.

She sobered. "Why do you think men *are* such bastards?"

"Now that's a question women have been asking since the beginning of time." Alex raised her hands expressively and let them fall. "I certainly can't answer it."

"I suppose I am generalizing." Jo sighed. "They can't all be as bad as Ben, otherwise every woman would be getting a divorce." Her eyes danced as Alex watched her, a small smile playing around her mouth. "Now that would be something of a statement, wouldn't it? If every woman suddenly filed for divorce. Talk about rumblings of mutiny." They both laughed together.

"But enough of me." Jo pushed Ben out of her mind. "I've been rambling on for ages. Tell me all about your week."

Alex shrugged. "Just your typical visit to the accountant. Nothing in the least dramatic. I'm afraid I can't match your impressive adventures."

They continued on to lighter topics, and eventually Alex suggested they move to sit in the lounge.

Jo sank down on the couch. Instead of taking the chair opposite, Alex sat down beside her, turning so that she was facing Jo. She refilled Jo's glass from the bottle of wine she'd brought with her from the table.

"I'm not sure this is such a good idea," Jo said, accepting the topping off of her glass with only token reluctance. "I usually have only one glass of wine."

"Even for celebratory purposes?" Alex asked lightly, setting the wine bottle on the floor.

"Absolutely. Wine has a tendency to go to my elbows and knees."

"That's better than having it go to your head."

"That's its next stop after the elbows and knees. In fact I'm feeling very laid back already."

"Are you likely to tell any deep dark secrets?"

Jo laughed. "I don't think I've got any. I told you I was totally boring." Jo took another sip of the wine, enjoying its cloying richness. "How about your secrets?"

Alex kept her gaze on her fingers as they played with the stem of her wineglass. "Oh, I've got plenty of those, but I think I'll probably need another glass or two."

Jo made a show of picking up the bottle of wine. "Then drink up," she said and giggled.

"Are you trying to get me drunk, Jo Creighton?" Alex asked with mock seriousness.

Jo giggled again. "I think I just might be."

"I'm warning you, you'll have to take the consequences."

"Consequences?" Jo repeated, her head on one side. "Will they be good or bad?"

Alex's dark eyes met hers, held her gaze for long moments. Jo imagined she could see herself reflected in the dusky pools, twin images that glowed in the dim light from the lamp. And she fancied she could drown in the fascination of their mysterious depths.

Jo's mouth went suddenly dry, and she swallowed. She couldn't seem to draw her eyes from Alex's.

"Good or bad? Well, that depends," Alex said huskily.

Jo swallowed again. "On what?" she asked, her voice a little thin to her ears.

Alex didn't reply. She slowly set down her glass of wine and leaned across to take Jo's glass from her nerveless fingers. Her eyes still holding Jo's she reached out, ran the tip of one finger lightly down the curve of Jo's cheek.

CHAPTER TWELVE

Jo's heart began to pound. The drumming rose inside her head, its beat so loud she thought it would deafen her. Surely Alex must hear it too?

Her entire body began to burn. Yet she couldn't move a muscle. Above the thunder of her heartbeats she recognized the clanging of her warning system, loudly demanding that she flee.

But she couldn't. Or wouldn't. Only her sybaritic senses clamored, sending slivers of pleasurable desire shafting from the point of contact of Alex's fingertip to each erogenous part of her body.

Alex leaned forward, and her full lips touched Jo's.

Desire exploded into a million tiny starbursts of sensation and Jo moaned as Alex's lips teased hers. When Alex drew slightly away, Jo's hungry mouth followed hers.

Jo felt as if she was drowning as the exquisite excitement magnified, multiplied, consumed her with a wild erotic craving.

Alex's tongue tip probed, and Jo willingly opened her lips. Alex's arms slid around her bare shoulders, pulled Jo firmly against her warm body.

As Jo's breasts touched Alex's, a shaft of desire shot through her. The intensity of her desire terrified Jo, and she pushed against Alex's shoulder to put some space between them. Their eyes met.

Jo was gasping shallow, agitated breaths into her tortured lungs as a rush of pure horror took hold of her. What was she doing? She wasn't — She couldn't be —

With a sharp cry, Jo scrambled to her feet. Alex was slower to move. She reached to clasp Jo's hand, but Jo had sprung away out of reach.

"Oh, my God!" Jo got out brokenly as Alex stood up.

"Jo. Please —" she began but Jo took another couple of shaky steps away from her.

"No. I . . . No." She put her hand over her mouth. "I'm sorry. I, I have to go."

Jo turned, grabbed her bag from the small table by the door, ran outside, and flung herself into her car, subconsciously aware that Alex was calling her name. Reaching into her bag, her fingers fumbled for the keys, clutched at them, and eventually found the ignition. The car roared to life. With a slither in the gravel drive, she turned out onto the road.

Jo didn't give any conscious thought to the direction she chose, but she instinctively eased her foot from the accelerator as the car sped down a winding hill. Before she knew it she was driving into Maleny, and without realizing it she turned and drove into the parking lot behind the hotel.

In daylight the building was unpretentious and low set, painted in earthy tones, but tonight it was a glowing oasis in the darkness. Light streamed with the noise through the open windows, and the rowdiness, the general bonhomie beckoned her.

It felt like midnight. But it couldn't be. The hotel was obviously still doing a roaring trade, and the sound of the reveling patrons spilled out onto the roadway. In the artificial light she glanced at her watch. Nine o'clock. Early really.

On rubbery legs Jo walked up to the door and into the lounge bar. She blinked in the artificial brightness and flinched at the intensified noise level.

Go home, a tiny voice inside advised her, but she shrugged that thought aside. No. Not to the empty flat. She couldn't bear to be alone. She didn't want to have to think about . . .

She pushed through the crowd to the bar and ordered a beer. With that in her hand she turned, her eyes seeking a table, a spare chair in the midst of the laughing, drinking crowd.

She raised the schooner to her lips and took a gulp and then another, and before she knew it she'd finished the glass. Without thinking she turned to the barman and ordered another. As she lifted it off the bar someone jostled her arm, and a liberal amount of the amber liquid splashed down the front of her dress.

Just then she spied a chair and made her way to it, sinking onto the seat. She rested her elbow on the table only to draw back in distaste at the sticky surface. She swallowed another mouthful of beer, and a churning in her stomach made her aware of the bitter taste of the drink. She shuddered slightly. She didn't even like beer. What was she doing here?

Alex's face swam before her eyes. Her high cheekbones, dark eyes, dark hair. The sensual curve of her mouth. She felt the softness of those full lips on hers, and that same knot of desire twisted inside her.

Oh, God! Oh, God! Jo moaned softly. What had she done? What had she said to lead Alex to even think Jo wanted ...?

She wasn't ... She'd never even wondered about ... about women. Women together.

Then she remembered the dreams, the waking to a feeling of sensual well-being, to the hazy memory of the heat of a warm sensuous body. A body like Alex's. Moving over her.

No! It was just a dream. Dreams were just that. You didn't act on them. Yet Alex's kiss had felt so right.

But she'd never been attracted to women.
Not until now!

Oh God! Her mind shied away from that thought in dire terror. She wasn't attracted to Alex. Not in that way. It was just ... She admired her. She recognized that Alex was an attractive woman, but ...

"Well now. Hi there. Don't try and tell me you're all alone, because I wouldn't believe my luck."

Jo looked up, brought the man standing in front of her into a hazy focus. Her head felt more than a little woozy, and she blinked to steady the slight tilt of the room.

The man hooked his booted foot around the leg of an empty chair behind him and swung it around so he could straddle it, one arm resting along the back, the other hand holding a mug of beer.

He needs a shave, Jo thought inconsequentially, or maybe he's growing a beard. He had dark hair, too, a little long, but it was clean enough, and he was tanned and muscular, the short sleeves of his shirt straining over his biceps. And suddenly he looked vaguely familiar.

"I haven't seen you here at the pub before or I would have remembered," the man was saying with a smile, his eyes flicking over Jo's breasts. "But we've met, haven't we?"

The man's arrogance struck a chord in Jo and then she remembered. "You're Des, the motorcycle mechanic."

He smiled broadly. "Once seen never forgotten, hey? What's your name, darling?"

"Jo," she said, and her voice seemed to be coming from some distance away from her. I'm not your darling, she wanted to scream at the man, but the words stuck in her throat. She took another mouthful of her beer.

"Jo? Well. Hello, Jo." The man grinned. "I see you've nearly finished your drink. How's about I get you a refill?"

"No. Thanks. I've had enough." More than enough, she told herself derisively.

Des drained his own glass. "Me too. So what

about a dance?" He reached out, took Jo's hand and drew her, unresisting, to her feet.

"No." Jo pulled against his hold, but he simply hauled the two of them through the crowd and into the room where lights flashed and a band played something loud and unrecognizable.

He turned and propelled Jo into his arms, held her hard against him, and began moving his feet in some step Jo hadn't a hope of following, had she wanted to.

She'd have to get away. Go home. Coming here had definitely been a huge mistake.

"This is cozy, isn't it?" The man yelled over the music.

Jo almost gagged on the smell of beer on his breath. "Actually, I'm rather tired, and the music's a little loud for me." Jo pulled away from the man's hold.

He drew her back. "Can't hear you, darling," he yelled back and swung her around.

The room spun dizzily, and Jo drew a steadying breath, clutching at the man for support. He started gyrating his hips suggestively against her. With horror, she felt the hardness of his erection. Jo pushed agitatedly against him, held her breasts back from the man's chest.

"I need some fresh air," she yelled at him.

He grinned. "Good idea. Let's go."

Once again Jo felt herself manhandled through the crush of people, and then she was outside, the cool night air momentarily reviving her. To Jo's horror, he nuzzled the side of her neck, bit her earlobe.

"You know, I had you pegged wrong, darling," he said huskily. "I thought you were a lezzie like Alex."

The man's wet lips were on hers, and Jo was momentarily paralyzed with shock before she began to struggle feverishly.

"What's the problem?" he asked belligerently.

"I —" Jo drew in a panicked breath, part of her recognizing the need to defuse this touchy situation. This man was strong, and she doubted she could fight him off if he chose to force himself on her. "I just need to go to the ladies room," she said quickly and made herself smile ruefully.

"Oh." The man slowly released her. "No doubt about you bloody women," he said with barely disguised impatience. "I'll get a beer and meet you back here. Okay?"

"All right." Jo made herself walk in the direction of her car.

"Hey! It's this way." The man indicated the other end of the building.

Jo paused, walked back past him, and continued walking for a few steps before turning back in time to see him disappear inside. She ran into the darkness, not knowing how little time she had to reach her own car. Keeping to the least lit areas she began working her way back to the other side of the parking lot.

She was a few cars away from her own when she heard her name called.

"Jo? Where the hell are you?"

The sound was coming from her right and she wondered if he'd have the gall to go into the ladies' rest room in search of her. She hid behind a dark

Ford as she listened to the man searching for her, calling her name.

Then there was silence, and she cautiously peeped around the car. She saw him standing near the door. He seemed undecided about what to do. Then he swore colorfully and returned to the pub.

Jo kept behind the cars as she continued around the parking lot. Her legs were still shaking as she found her small sedan.

She started to unlock the door but shook her head. How many drinks had she actually had? Two? Three? No matter. On top of the wine she'd had earlier, she had to be well over the limit. She was in no condition to drive safely.

She rubbed her arms at the coolness of the night breeze and tried to decide what she should do. As she stood there feeling nauseous a taxi pulled up to the back of the pub and two couples tumbled out, heading in the direction of the noisy carousing.

Jo stepped quickly up to the now empty cab and clasped the door to steady herself. "Are you for hire?" she asked thickly.

"Sure am, lady. Hop in."

Jo sank into the sagging backseat, buckling herself in as the driver asked her where she wanted to go. She mumbled the address and rested her head against the seat, closing her weary eyes.

She must have dozed, for the sound of the crunch of tires on gravel woke her with a start. She fumbled in her bag, paid the driver, and she was out on the driveway. The taxi had driven away before she realized she must have given Alex's address. She stood uncertainly gazing at the house.

The subdued light of the lamp still burned in the

living room, and Jo agitatedly twisted the strap of her bag in her cold fingers.

She'd have to use Alex's phone to call another cab. And apart from that, she acknowledged, she shouldn't have run off the way she had. She should have stayed, explained to Alex that she wasn't gay, that she wanted Alex as a friend. She owed Alex that much.

Before she could think about what she was doing, she walked shakily up to the door and knocked tentatively. There was no answer. She tried the doorknob. The door opened to her touch, and she drew a deep breath and stepped inside.

"Alex?" she said, her voice high and thin.

She continued into the living room. The table set so intimately was just as it was when she'd left, the remains of their meal untouched. She moved farther into the room.

Jo glanced uneasily at the stairs. Would Alex have gone to bed and left the door unlocked? Surely not.

A breeze stirred the leaves of the potted fern on the breakfast bar, and Jo noticed that the sliding glass door to the deck was open. She swallowed, her throat tender, as she stepped outside.

In the moonlight Alex's figure was silhouetted against the night sky. She was leaning against the veranda post, one hand resting on the railing.

"Alex?" Jo's voice was husky, the word catching in her throat, her heartbeats quickened in her chest.

The other woman didn't move. Only the tightening of her fingers on the railings gave Jo any indication that she was aware of Jo's presence.

"Alex, I . . ." Jo took a couple of tentative steps toward her. "Alex, I'm sorry. I should have, I mean I shouldn't have . . . run off like that. I guess I . . ." She gulped on a half sob.

Alex turned then, one strong hand making a movement toward Jo. But then she let it fall, thrust it into the pocket of her slacks. "No, don't. You don't have to explain," Alex said tightly, her voice sounding impossibly deeper.

"I'm sorry," Jo said again, not knowing what to do. Alex swore softly under her breath.

"I'm the one who should be apologizing, Jo," she bit out. "I made a mistake." She gave a soft, bitter laugh. "One of the biggest of my life. I never should have . . ." She moved her hand negatingly. "I would never have done anything to spoil our friendship. I just . . ." She stopped and shrugged. "Put it down to too much wine."

"I guess we both had too much of that," Jo said, clutching at the excuse, yet knowing deep inside her that it was just that, a handy excuse. "It was just a misunderstanding," she added. She heard Alex sigh.

"Yes. A misunderstanding." Alex paused. "Look, Jo. I don't know why exactly, but just lately I thought you'd realized I was gay."

"I never really thought about it." Jo swallowed guiltily. "Well, not consciously. You said you'd been married."

Alex's mouth twisted. "In my case that doesn't mean anything. I've lived as a lesbian for about seventeen years. I think I'm relatively open about it. Or, at least, I don't try to hide it."

"I —" Jo stopped and her stomach churned again. The beer she'd had on top of the wine she'd already drunk at dinner shifted unsettledly inside her, and she felt decidedly nauseous. What if she was sick in front of Alex. She put one hand to her mouth and swayed giddily.

Alex was beside her in a moment. "What's the matter? Come on inside." She took Jo's arm, led her into the lamp-lit living room. "You look as if you need to sit down."

Jo felt cold and clammy. As the light from the kitchen hit her, she closed her eyes, her head pounding again.

Alex said something Jo couldn't quite catch, and then she was helping Jo up the stairs, through the bedroom and into the en suite. Jo sank down onto the toilet, and Alex ran some cold water on a face washcloth, wringing it out and holding it on Jo's forehead.

"How's that?" Alex asked gently. "Feel any better?"

Jo started to nod her head and then grimaced. "A little." She drew a breath and made a face again. "I smell like a brewery, don't I? I think I spilled some beer on my dress."

"Beer? Where on earth have you been?" Alex asked as she wiped Jo's face.

"The pub. In Maleny."

"If you drank beer on top of the wine, it's no wonder you feel like death."

"I think I had a couple. Maybe they were shandies. I don't know. I can't usually drink beer." Jo opened her eyes. "I'm sorry, Alex. I should have just gone home. I must have given the taxi driver your address by mistake."

"I'm glad you did. I'd have been so worried about you. I tried to ring your flat and kept getting no answer. I wasn't sure if you were there and not answering or, worse still, not there. I was tossing up whether or not I should go and see."

"Oh, God." Jo moaned. "I feel awful."

She started to stand up and then had to grope for the toilet bowl. Alex held her head. When Jo had finished, Alex sponged her clammy face. Alex ran the washcloth under the tap again and returned it to Jo's forehead.

"Okay now?" she asked gently.

"I think so." Jo swallowed. "Oh, Alex. I'm so sorry." Jo cringed in mortification that Alex had to see her like this.

"Don't worry, Jo. Here, hold this against your forehead and I'll get you a clean towel. A shower might help, and getting out of those clothes and away from the smell of the beer."

Jo groaned and sat down again until Alex returned. "Towel and clean nightshirt. Do you think you'll be able to manage by yourself?" she asked levelly. Jo couldn't meet her gaze.

"Yes. I . . . I think so. Thanks."

"Right. Just call me if you want anything."

Alex left her, and Jo slowly stood up. She moved gingerly to stand in front of the mirror over the wash basin, and she groaned softly again. She looked like death warmed over.

What a fool she was. None of this would have happened if she hadn't bolted like a startled colt when Alex kissed her, she berated herself ruthlessly. An adult would have stayed, explained to Alex that she had made a mistake, that she wasn't interested in a physical relationship. She just wanted to be Alex's friend.

Jo met her own gaze in the mirror. A stab of

emotion surged through her, that same so terrifying torrent of physical desire that had overwhelmed her at the first touch of Alex's lips.

She touched her lips with shaking fingers and winced with guilty remorse. It was scarcely Alex's fault that she had misinterpreted Jo's message. For Jo had most certainly not immediately repulsed Alex.

She had kissed Alex back with more passion than she'd ever imagined she was capable of. She'd certainly never responded to Ben's kiss like that.

And if she were honest she'd have to admit it was as much the shock of her response to Alex's kiss as the fact that Alex had actually kissed her that had made her flee so impetuously.

So how was she going to explain that to Alex? When she scarcely knew how to explain it to herself. She turned away from her pale features and fumbled blindly for the zipper on her dress. She stood in the shower and let the water cascade over her for ages, and then she made herself step out, dry herself off.

She slipped Alex's nightshirt over her head, and the soft material flowed over her body. She put her hand on her stomach, and her mouth went dry. It was quivering again but not in the same way, not from the effects of the alcohol.

Sudden flashes of images from her dream swam ethereally before her eyes. Her naked body. And Alex.

Jo's nipples hardened; she crossed her arms over them, trying to tell herself it was the change in temperature and not the thought of Alex.

Hastily she used some of Alex's toothpaste to rinse her mouth out and, taking a steadying breath, she tentatively opened the door and stepped into Alex's bedroom.

CHAPTER THIRTEEN

The room was large and airy, the timber rafters in the sloping ceiling exposed and stained to a rich brown, contrasting with the cream-colored walls. The floor was highly polished timber, too, with thick scatter rugs on either side of the queen-size bed.

Jo turned her gaze from the bed and walked slowly across to the open window. She could just make out the ragged outlines of the Glasshouse Mountains. She drew in a deep breath of the clear air before turning back to the room.

A large photograph caught her eye. It was bigger

than the one on the wall downstairs, but Jo knew instinctively it was taken by the same photographer. The subject was the same, too. Jo crossed to stand closer, and she felt her skin prickle as that same heat crept over her body.

This time Alex was completely nude. She had her back to the camera, had turned slightly to look over her shoulder at the photographer, one arm holding up a tangle of dark hair. And the clever lighting etched the shadowy shape of her body. The rounded curve of her so feminine hip. The hint of the indentation of a dimple just below her waist at the back. Her smooth square shoulder. And the tantalizing swell of one full breast.

Jo drew her gaze from that and looked at the profile of Alex's face, the outline of her strong jaw, straight nose, her soft lips and those dark, burning eyes. Of its own volition, Jo's hand went out, her fingers tracing the clearly highlighted lines of Alex's body. She touched her hip, her waist, lingered sensually on her breast. And Jo swallowed, trying to ease the ache in her chest.

Finally she put her fingers to Alex's mouth, paused, and then brought her fingers to her own lips, as though to relive, to memorize that exquisite moment when Alex had kissed her.

Those same spirals of desire exploded inside her, and she turned away from the photograph, panicked by the depth of her response. On shaking legs she crossed to the large bed and sank down onto the side of it.

Alex must have folded the thick calico spread onto the end of the bed, and she'd turned back the crisp cotton sheets. Jo desperately wanted to relax on the bed, close her eyes, feel Alex slide into the bed beside her. Yet she couldn't allow that. As much as she wanted to.

She saw herself standing on the edge of a deep and deliciously dangerous chasm and knew she had to make a conscious decision. To turn and walk away or to fall forward into the abyss. If she took that irretrievable step forward, even in her befuddled state, she knew there would be no going back, that her life would be changed forever.

Jo closed her eyes and ran a hand over her throbbing head only to start at the sound of soft footsteps on the stairs. Alex's head appeared, and then her shoulders, her chest, her waist, her rounded hips. Jo watched her as she approached. As she drew closer Jo's heart seemed to beat faster.

Take that step forward, her body screamed at her, as desire seemed to radiate from every pore in her skin.

"Feel any better?" Alex asked lightly, and Jo tried to nod, flinching as her head throbbed anew.

"A little. I guess I deserve a massive hangover," she said dejectedly.

Alex laughed softly and walked closer. "I don't see that that will make you feel any better right now. Why don't you lie back. Relax." She started to put her hand on Jo's shoulder, and Jo jumped instinctively.

"I'm sorry," Jo muttered, a flush of humiliation coloring her neck and face. "I'm just —"

"Exhausted?" Alex finished, and Jo nodded, letting Alex push her gently back onto the pillow.

She slid her legs under the sheet, and Alex pulled the sheet up to her chin. Then she sat on the edge of the bed and smoothed Jo's hair back from her face.

"A good night's sleep is what you want."

Jo blinked up at her. "What are . . . ? I mean, what about you?"

"Me, too," Alex agreed. "I'll see you in the morning." She stood up to walk back toward the stairs.

"But where? Aren't you . . . ?" Jo slid a quick glance at the other side of the bed and swallowed disconcertedly. "Aren't you going to sleep here?" she got out in a rush.

Alex sighed and came back to sit on the edge of the bed again. "I think it's best that I sleep downstairs." She lifted Jo's hand, rubbed gently at her palm.

"I . . ." Jo gulped. "I wouldn't mind if you did . . . sleep with me, Alex," she stammered, barely able to meet Alex's eyes.

"And I'm not saying I don't want," Alex paused, "to sleep with you, Jo. I do." She made a self-derogatory face. "But I'm not sure I could just sleep with you. If you were that close to me tonight, I'd want more. And that would be breaking a Farmer Golden Rule, the one pertaining to making love to inebriated women."

Jo blushed again as Alex's dark eyes held her gaze.

"When I make love to a woman, I want her to be stone-cold sober. Or perhaps a little drunk on the

147

passion of the moment. I want my lover to make her own decision and know that it's me she's sleeping with. No excuses in the morning, no recriminations."

She leaned slowly forward, kissed Jo softly on the lips, and turned and left. "Goodnight, Jo."

Jo watched her go, blinked into the darkness when Alex flicked off the light. As her eyes became accustomed to the gloom, she glanced across to the window and then at the photograph.

The shaft of weak moonlight coming in the window made the photograph almost discernible, but Jo really didn't need the light. She rather suspected she had that picture of Alex burned indelibly into her memory. As she turned over to hug the spare pillow, the picture stayed with her as she drifted off to sleep.

Before Jo woke the next morning, Alex had ridden her bike down to the pub and driven Jo's car back to the house. Jo spent long, strained minutes avoiding Alex's gaze as she sat at the breakfast bar while Alex poured her a cup of coffee.

Then Alex sighed. "Look, Jo. We need to talk, but I know you're in no fit state to do that right now. So. I think it would be best to put some space between us."

Jo's heart contracted painfully, and hot tears stung behind her eyes. Did Alex mean she didn't want to see her any more? Suddenly her days stretched ahead with a dreadful emptiness.

"Last night," Alex was continuing, "was pretty harrowing for you." Her lips twisted wryly. "For both of us. And I think you need some time to get everything into perspective. I really value your friendship, Jo, and I'll admit I don't want to lose that."

"Neither do I," Jo said thickly, sincerely.

"I'd like you to take a few days to think about, well, everything, and then maybe we can have a talk about all this more rationally. Okay?"

Jo nodded. "Okay. I'm sorry."

Alex held up her hand. "No more remorse or self-reproach. If you've finished your coffee I'll get you to drop me down at the pub so I can pick up my bike."

They were silent on the short journey down to the hotel. Alex climbed from the car and turned back to Jo. "I'll give you a ring in a few days."

Jo nodded.

Then Alex had straightened and was striding across to her motorcycle.

For two days Jo tortured herself with what might have been, with thoughts of painful loss and electrifying promises of surrendering to the ache inside her to feel Alex's arms around her again.

When Mike had knocked on her door on Sunday afternoon she had pleaded a migraine, warning him it could last for days. He commiserated and thankfully left her alone. So when there was another rap on her door on Monday afternoon, she fully expected it to be Mike calling to see how she was. But it was Ben.

Jo stared at him in disbelief, and he held up his hands in a demonstration of capitulation.

"I come bearing abject apologies," he said with his most charming grin.

"Ben —"

He let his hands fall. "I mean it, Jo. I was, well, out of line last week. I guess I was feeling down, and I'd had a couple too many drinks." He shrugged.

Jo could identify with the too many drinks, she thought ironically, and her stomach clenched in memory. She sighed and nodded. "All right, Ben. Apology accepted."

His smile broadened. "Great. Can I come in? I have some papers for you to look over," he added quickly at her skeptical look.

"As long as you keep your hands to yourself." Jo reluctantly stood back, and Ben picked up his briefcase and stepped inside.

"I guess I deserved that. I'm sorry, Jo. You know I'm not usually so crass." He opened his briefcase. "I'll leave the papers with you so there's no rush," he said as he slid the large manilla envelope out onto the table. "I could have let the lawyers handle it, but I did want to apologize. I've felt like a heel all weekend."

"You acted like a heel, Ben," Jo said succinctly. Before Ben could reply, the doorbell jangled loudly. They both jumped.

For long moments both she and Ben froze like statues, and then Jo made herself turn away, cross to the door. When she pulled it open she could barely take in the jean-clad figure standing facing her.

"Hi!" said Alex lightly. "I was committed to ringing that doorbell before I remembered how loud it was."

Alex wore a pair of faded jeans and the same soft, blue chambray shirt she'd worn once before, the cuffs rolled back to just below her elbows.

"Oh. Alex. Hello." Jo swallowed quickly, unable to think of anything except the remembered feel of Alex's lips on her own. The knot of remembered desire that had been teasing her mercilessly for the past two days resurfaced with a vengeance, and she had to fight an almost overwhelming longing to throw herself into Alex's arms.

Then a hand descended on Jo's shoulder.

"Who is it, darling?" Ben asked easily, and Jo watched as Alex's dark eyes went from herself to Ben to the familiarity of his hand on her shoulder. Jo couldn't move. Her brain seemed to have gone into dead slow mode.

Although physically Ben was a few inches taller than Alex her whole deportment seemed to dwarf him. Jo suspected Ben sensed that, for he drew himself up to his full height.

Jo glanced at him in time to see him boldly assessing Alex, his eyes settling suggestively and openly on her full breasts.

"If you're selling something —" Ben began and Jo moved jerkily, trying to free herself from his proprietary hand but she was up against the door.

"No," she said quickly, and Ben's hand slid to the small of her back. "Ben, this is Alex Farmer, my friend who took the photo. Alex, this is my ex-husband, Ben."

"Ah. The photographer." Ben turned on his smile.

Alex silently inclined her head. Although she made no comment, she left Ben in no doubt her acknowledgment was perfunctory.

Knowing how sarcastically unpleasant he became when he suspected a slight, imagined or otherwise, force of habit had Jo trying valiantly to think of something to say to diffuse Ben's anger.

"Nice picture you took of Jo," Ben said, his tone all condescension. "You made that plain little face of hers look almost beautiful."

"I think she is beautiful," Alex remarked evenly.

Ben laughed. "Well, she's cute. But we wouldn't say beautiful, would we, Jo? Interesting hobby though, photography," he continued before Jo could comment.

"Alex is a professional photographer." Jo found her voice.

"Do you make much money taking pictures?"

Alex shrugged as Jo cringed. "On and off." She glanced at Jo again as Ben slid his arm around Jo's waist.

"Alex, I —"

"It's all right, Jo," Alex said, not meeting Jo's eyes. "I was going to be passing by and thought I'd drop off these books for you." She held out two books. With a totally reflex action, Jo took them.

"Thank you," she said, her voice thick.

Alex gave a faint nod of her head. "I'll see you then."

"Ben was just going," Jo got out quickly, desperate for Alex to stay.

"Now, Jo. Don't hold the lady up." Ben tightened his grip on her waist, bringing her closer to his side, and Jo turned to him with an angry glare. He slowly released her.

"You don't have to go, Alex," Jo said levelly.

Alex gave her a faint smile. "I know," she said and with one last look at Ben she turned on her heel and strode out along the driveway.

Jo wanted to run after her.

"That was a *big* woman," Ben exclaimed as Jo slowly turned from the door. "I wouldn't want to run into her in a dark alley." He cocked his head and read the titles on the spines of the books Jo still held in her nerveless fingers. "Poetry? Give me a break! She looks like she'd be into all that ardent feminist trash."

Jo set the books on the coffee table and turned back to face him.

"I think you'd better go, Ben."

"Oh, come on, Jo. I said I was sorry about the other day. And I could use a drink. You make great coffee. We could talk."

"I don't think we have anything to say. About anything. Do what you like with the house. I couldn't care less."

"What about the papers?"

Jo shrugged. "I'll read them and get back to the attorney when I have time."

Ben regarded her petulantly. "You really have changed. More than I thought. And now I think I see why. How long have you known that, that Farmer woman?"

"Not long. What's that got to do with anything?"

"That woman's been brainwashing you, hasn't she?" he said bitingly, speaking over Jo's negation.

"She's been filling you with all this women's rights shit."

"You don't suppose I could have changed on my own, Ben?" Jo said with sarcasm. "Or perhaps I should say, waked up to myself. And I happen to think women do need more rights."

"Oh, spare me!" Ben exclaimed. "You were happy enough with your lot before."

"Was I?"

"Yes, you were." Ben snatched up his briefcase. "In my experience, someone like you would need some coaching. And I can see where you got it. Women like her make me sick. They're too unattractive to get their own men, so they try to make normal women dissatisfied."

"Ben, that's —"

"Why do you think society's in such a bad way?" he continued as though she hadn't spoken. "It started going downhill when women went out to work. They should be home looking after their husbands and kids. We're all getting totally bored with all you women crying, 'Poor us!' You should be facing up to your own failures, not blaming everything on men." He gave Jo a look of disdain. "But I'm surprised you'd even be part of it, Jo."

"I seem to recall you were happy for me to be working, Ben."

"That was only until we got on our feet. If we'd had kids, you'd have been at home looking after them."

"Would I have?"

"Of course you would."

"We'll never know, will we?" Jo folded her arms. "Good-bye, Ben."

He stood watching her, high spots of color in his cheeks, the usual sign of his anger at being thwarted. "Oh, this Farmer woman has really been a good influence on you, I can see that. I wouldn't mind betting she'd as dykey as they come."

Jo felt hot color wash her cheeks, and Ben's gaze narrowed again.

"Maybe that's it, is it, Jo?" He snapped his fingers. "I thought it was that blond, muscle-bound guy, but I think I had the wrong end of the stick. Has that woman been broadening your horizons?"

"I don't know what you mean," Jo began, her heartbeats fluttering anxiously.

"Was that why you gave me the cold shoulder last week? Has that dyke broad been tickling your fancy, Jo?"

Jo raised her chin, her jaw tight with anger. She wanted to lash out at him, defend Alex. But she knew Ben of old. Rushing to Alex's defense would only make things worse. If they could be any worse.

"Wouldn't that be the joke of the century?" Ben was elatedly asking himself. "My so prim and proper little wife dabbling in the sins of lesbian flesh."

"That's enough, Ben. You've had your sordid little joke. Alex is a good friend of mine. And whatever choices I make these days, well, the decisions are mine."

"Is she better at getting you going than I am? No wonder you were such a dead loss in bed."

"Good-bye, Ben," Jo repeated evenly and gestured toward the open door.

With one final scathing look, Ben turned and left the flat. Jo slammed the door behind him.

She sank down onto the couch, reaching over to

pick up Alex's poetry books, clasping them to her. Eventually she glanced at the titles and she smiled faintly. *The Romantics.*

Jo sat there for ages, hugging the books to her chest, her mind replaying a profusion of pictures of Alex. Alex glaring down on her that first morning. Alex at the craft shop, quietly pleased with Jo's choices. Alex adjusting her camera as she took Jo's photograph. Alex astride her motorcycle. Alex across the table from her on Saturday night, the candlelight giving her dark eyes that immeasurably deep, mysterious glow.

And she felt Alex's lips on her own, soft as pure silk.

Alex had obviously called to talk, but Ben's appearance and his dreadful behavior had driven her away. What if Alex thought . . . ?

Jo sprang to her feet and the books fell to the floor. She only gave them a cursory glance as she reached for her car keys and ran out of the flat.

What if Alex thought Jo was in any way reconciled with Ben? Jo almost groaned in despair. Surely Alex wouldn't think that. But what if she did?

Jo became so agitated she clutched at the steering wheel and the car swerved. Her stomach quivered, and her whole body began to shake. She slowed the car and pulled off the winding road onto the narrow shoulder.

Why was it so important what Alex thought? Jo's mouth went dry at the answer she tried not to allow herself to formulate.

Alex was her friend, she told herself quickly. She'd feel bad about something like that happening with any friend, wouldn't she? And Alex was a better friend than most.

Alex was more than a friend. Jo's mouth went dry as the thought crystallized. Yes, Alex was more than a friend, she acknowledged, and her fingers relaxed a little, released their painful grasp on the steering wheel.

Jo swallowed. But did she want that? The question screamed inside her. And the dreams. The warmth, the evocative sensuality, the merging of two souls.

Were the dreams her subconscious mind telling her there were other options? That the elusive happiness she seemed to have been seeking for years was so obviously within her grasp?

She sat there trying to rationally sort out her answer. Yet everything came back to Alex. Alex's kiss. The way it made her feel.

Her mind thrust forward the *againsts* while her heart just repeated one *for*. She was in love with Alex.

But society. Her family. Her job. People she knew. What would they think?

She was in love with Alex. And what was she going to do about it?

Eventually Jo started the car and continued the drive to Alex's house, a journey that seemed endless yet seemed to take no time at all. Then she was turning down the steep driveway and pulling up in front of the house.

Jo rapped on the door and waited with a sense of déjà vu as her knock went unanswered. She reached out and turned the knob, stepping inside.

Jo's eyes went immediately to the deck, and she saw Alex leaning on the railing, looking out over the panorama as the shadows lengthened. She walked across the floor, paused in the doorway, and the answer she was seeking suddenly became as clear as a shallow mountain stream.

"Alex?" she said softly, and Alex straightened, turned slowly.

Jo took a couple of steps forward, stopped a few paces away from her.

Jo swallowed. "Thank you again for the books?" she said inanely, her heart thudding madly in her chest.

Alex smiled crookedly. "I wasn't sure you'd want to read them."

"Oh, I do. I wanted to . . ." Jo's voice faltered again. "I didn't want you to think that I, that Ben and I had . . ." Her voice completely died on her.

"I didn't think that," Alex said quietly.

"Oh. That's good. I, I also wanted to tell you I've been thinking and . . . About the other night. I wanted to explain. About my . . ." Jo swallowed painfully again. "About why I responded. When you kissed me."

Alex made a movement with her hand. "It's all right, Jo. You don't have to do this. I know what it was."

"Do you?" Jo asked quietly.

Alex ran a hand over her eyes and Jo saw her fingers were shaking slightly.

"I know what it was, too, Alex," she said steadily. Voicing it seemed to have a strengthening effect on her. She straightened and took the few remaining steps toward Alex's taut body, stopping a mere arm's length from her. "I know what it was," she repeated huskily, and the sound of Alex's sharply indrawn breath dispelled the last vestige of Jo's uncertainty.

CHAPTER FOURTEEN

Jo slowly lifted her hand and touched the softness of Alex's cheek, then gently, her mouth. "I couldn't believe that lips could be so soft," she said thickly. "When you kissed me, a whole world of sensations that had been churning inside me all fell into place. The most perfect place.

"Everything came into sharp focus. That day when I met you in the craft shop, after you left, I knew what the girl in the craft shop, Cindy's, familiarity meant.

"And Mrs. Craven. She always gave out dire

warnings every time I mentioned you." Jo smiled shakily. "I let it all drift over my head. But deep inside I knew. I wouldn't admit it, but I knew. Only in my dreams did I allow myself to feel it."

Alex's dark eyes hadn't left hers, and Jo swallowed quickly. "I've always found everything difficult when it came to socializing, to communicating. I've always been scared."

Alex closed her eyes, took hold of Jo's hand, placed a soft kiss on her fingers. "There's nothing to be afraid of, Jo. Not now. And not from me. I'm willing to let you take your time, get used to this. We can talk if you like."

"I think we need to do that." Jo gave a self-derisive laugh. "I'm sure we do. But right this minute I think I might go mad if you don't kiss me again, like you did the other night."

Alex's full mouth curved into a quick smile and then it faded and she lowered her head, her lips touching Jo's with exquisite tenderness. She placed quick kisses on both corners of Jo's mouth, pulled away to look deeply into her eyes again.

Jo's breath caught in her throat before escaping on a low moan.

Alex touched soft kisses to Jo's eyelids, her nose, her cheekbones, almost the corner of her mouth. Jo felt as though she'd literally stopped breathing. She was consumed by a burning fever, her face feeling as though it was incandescent.

Alex nibbled her earlobe and Jo's muscles tensed excitedly, her nerve endings sending tingling signals all over her hot body.

After centuries Alex's lips slid back toward Jo's mouth. When their lips finally met, Jo drowned in timeless sensation as Alex's lips claimed hers in the kiss Jo had been reliving in her waking moments and dreaming about in her sleep.

She was adrift, clinging only to Alex's soft, enticing lips, as waves of pure desire seemed to explode inside her, rage through her like a bushfire before a westerly wind.

Jo slid her arms around Alex's neck. They clung together, bodies melding, thigh to thigh, stomach to stomach, breast to breast. When they finally drew apart they were both breathless.

"Oh, God!" Jo breathed unevenly. "I thought I'd dreamed it was so good. But I didn't. It was just as wonderful as I remembered."

Alex laughed softly, her hands sliding down to Jo's hips, holding her firmly against her own body.

Standing on tiptoe, Jo began touching Alex's face with warm kisses. "I just want to keep doing this. I never want to stop." She snuggled against Alex's softness, her face in the curve of Alex's neck, her lips tasting, caressing the warm skin.

Alex's hands came up to cradle Jo's face, one thumb brushing gently against Jo's sensitive lips. Jo trembled against her. "And I don't want you to stop either," Alex murmured huskily.

She drew a deep breath. Her breasts brushed Jo's, sending spirals of instantaneous yearning arrowing downward toward Jo's thighs.

Alex moaned softly and reluctantly moved a little away from Jo. "Let's sit down, otherwise my legs just might give out on me."

She took Jo's hand, led her inside, and started to cross to the couch. Alex paused, looked at the stairs and then at Jo, her eyes darkening with an unspoken question.

Jo lifted Alex's hand holding hers, kissed it gently, and moved them toward the stairs. Alex caught her breath and then led the way. Jo followed her. Would have followed her anywhere.

In the bedroom, Alex switched on the bedside lamp, sending a warm glow into the dusky shadows. She turned and sank onto the bed, gently drawing Jo down beside her. She lowered her lips to Jo's, and her kiss to Jo was a lingering promise of barely imagined delight.

She ran her fingertip gently over Jo's nose, traced her lips, journeyed downward to the neck of her T-shirt, stopped tantalizingly, and then continued slowly over the thin material to encircle first one of Jo's breasts and then the other. Even through the thickness of her shirt, at the touch of Alex's fingers Jo's nipples came instantly alert.

She arched against Alex's hand as, with painful slowness, Alex's teasing finger slid lower. Alex paused for long moments at the waistband of Jo's jeans, and a low moan escaped Jo's dry lips. She wanted to beg Alex not to stop, to let her fingers continue their erotic expedition. And when they did gently rub against the seam of Jo's jeans, Jo heard herself cry Alex's name with a deep huskiness she barely recognized as her own voice.

"You're trembling," Alex murmured softly as she raised her head.

Jo gave a nervous laugh. "I can't seem to stop."

"You're not afraid of me, are you?"

"No. Not of you." Jo assured her quickly.

Alex's dark brows rose. "Do you want to talk first?" she asked huskily.

Jo shook her head. "No," she said brokenly. "I think I said before I've been scared of most things all my life. Scared of new schools. Scared of teachers. A new job. Scared of passing a group of guys. Of doing things. Scared of, well, you name it. And now" — she shrugged in self-derision — "I've never been more terrified of anything in my life."

Alex took Jo's hand. "We don't have to do this you know. You can change your mind even now, if you want to."

"No." Jo impassionedly brought Alex's hand to her lips. "No. I might be scared, but I've never, I've never wanted anything more in my life before either."

Alex's dark eyes, black in the dim light, seemed to glow, and Jo's heart shifted in her breast. Alex lowered her head until her lips rested softly against Jo's forehead, then finally, her lips. Jo's breath caught in her chest as her heartbeats thundered in a mixture of apprehension and anticipation.

Jo's mouth opened, her tongue seeking Alex's, tantalizing the tender skin within. Her body seemed to sigh as they merged together.

Eons later they broke apart, both gasping deep uneven breaths, and Jo moaned, weakly resting her hot forehead against Alex's.

"Oh, God! I can't believe . . ." She sought Alex's lips again, tasting, teasing. "Your lips are so soft. Like" — Jo made a negating movement of her head — "I can't even begin to find an analogy." She kissed Alex again. "They're like soft whispers of fairy floss but not as intangible." She gave an embarrassed laugh. "I'm sorry. I seem to be getting carried away."

"I'd be devastated if you didn't, so get as carried away as you like." Alex laughed softly, and the low tone played over Jo's body like smooth warm oil on overheated skin. She leaned forward and kissed Alex again.

"I still don't seem to be able to stop doing this."

"And I still don't want you to stop," Alex said, and they kissed again.

Alex ran the tip of her finger gently down the planes of Jo's cheek, over her lips, pausing there. She smiled as Jo nibbled gently on her fingertip, then she retraced her path along Jo's jawline, encircled her ear, trailed down her throat, slowly followed the neckline of her shirt.

"I think we can dispense with this." Alex's deep voice continued to play over Jo like a delicate melody. Alex's hand reached for the bottom of Jo's shirt, and she lifted it over Jo's head. Her fingers went to the soft skin of Jo's midriff, moved upward, her strong hands cupping Jo's lace-covered breasts.

A kaleidoscope of wild desire almost engulfed Jo. She moaned, a raw, erotic sound she scarcely recognized as her own voice. She threw her head back, and Alex tenderly, urgently kissed the curve of Jo's throat.

Her lips then traced the line of Jo's lacy bra, her mouth settling in the hollow between her small breasts. Her fingers tantalized Jo's nipples until Jo had to stop herself from crying out, from begging Alex to stop. And not to stop.

Alex dispensed with Jo's bra, murmured appreciatively as Jo's naked breasts seemed to swell into her hands. And Jo's nipples hardened again, strained toward Alex's questing fingers. Memory stirred, and suddenly Jo tensed. Alex looked up at her, a small frown on her forehead.

"They're barely a handful," she said throatily, quoting Ben.

"They're more than perfect," Alex said thickly and lowered her head to take one rosy nipple in her mouth. Her lips and tongue gently teased, and Jo wound her fingers in Alex's short thick hair, cradling her head against her. Her breathing had quickened, and just when she thought she could bear no more Alex's lips returned to rest in the hollow between Jo's breasts.

Then Alex leaned back, her fingers sliding downward to the waistband of Jo's jeans. The stud came undone with a loud sound that echoed in the room. Their eyes met again.

"Okay?" Alex asked softly. "Last chance to turn around," she added lightly.

Jo nodded, reaching down to shakily slide her zipper downward. "I'm abiding by the Farmer Golden Rule, Alex. I'm sober and I've made my decision. And I know it's you I'm sleeping with."

Alex laughed her throaty laugh again. "My, I do believe we have something of a fast learner here," she said as she helped Jo out of her jeans.

"Now. Where were we?" Alex touched her lips to Jo's bare skin, tantalizing her nipples, moving downward, over her flat stomach, encircling her navel. "You taste delicious," she said. Her hand trailed lightly up the inside of Jo's thigh, her fingers slipping beneath the waistband of her bikini pants, sliding them downward.

Jo moved tentatively, and Alex looked up at her, dark eyes burning. Jo swallowed. "I'm sorry. I'm just —"

"Shy?" Alex finished, and Jo nodded. "Don't be. You're really beautiful. Your skin's so soft." Alex ran her hand lightly over the gentle curve of Jo's hips, returned to the tangle of light hair. "So is this," she added with a smile. And then her fingers slid gently into the soft damp folds, encircled, tantalized.

Jo moaned, arched her back toward Alex, felt her breasts brush against the material of Alex's shirt. With one shaking hand she managed to drag the back of Alex's shirt from the waistband of her jeans. She fumbled beneath the now loose shirt, searching for the clasp of Alex's bra. Then she remembered. Alex didn't wear one.

"Please, Alex. Help me," she murmured brokenly. "I want to feel you, too."

Her trembling fingers pulled at Alex's shirt, and she heard a button pop. Alex raised her head, her eyes crinkling at the corners.

"They don't make buttons like they used to, do they?" she asked, and Jo tried to laugh.

But her fingers were fumbling with the other buttons, undoing them. She was desperate to feel Alex's skin against hers. At last she pushed the shirt from Alex's shoulders. Jo could only gaze at the perfect fullness of Alex's breasts, and when she drew her eyes away Alex was watching her.

She smiled crookedly. "Well?"

"They're so beautiful," Jo said in awe, as she cupped Alex's breasts in her hands. "I never imagined a woman's body could be so beautiful. I want to bury my face in them." She looked up at Alex and blushed.

Alex slowly leaned over Jo, one hand on either side of her head, and she lowered herself until her large nipples were just brushing Jo's. Jo closed her eyes, lost herself in the feel of Alex's softness. Then she opened her eyes, moved down a little, and took one hardened nipple into her mouth, and then the other.

"My God! You're, oh, Alex." With a low moan Jo pressed herself against Alex, tasting her, drawing in the sweet smell of Alex's skin. "Now I know why men like women with large breasts."

Alex gave a husky laugh, her face still flushed. "Not all men do," she said.

"If I was a man I would."

"May I just say I'm glad you do and I'm very glad you're not."

They laughed softly together, and then Jo sobered, her fingers drawn back to the wonderful feel of Alex's skin. One finger encircled one nipple, and she took the other in her mouth. Alex expelled a ragged breath, sending shivers of delighted pleasure coursing through Jo.

Alex made a noise deep in her throat, and her fingers returned to Jo to tease again, moving into the damp soft curls, eliciting Jo's moaning in response.

In a split second of revelation, memories of Jo's dream returned. She was naked, aroused, and Alex was moving over her. Her whole body tingled, each nerve ending dancing, sending a stimulating message careering about her body. She was alive, and it all fell so rightly, so wonderfully, into place.

"Alex." She breathed the other woman's name into the softness of Alex's body, felt herself open, raising her hips to meet Alex's hand. Her stomach slid against the cloth of Alex's jeans. Her breasts swelled, nipples hardening as they slid against Alex's.

Alex's fingers took the rhythm from Jo's movements, slid into her wetness, caressing, inciting. The fire built inside Jo, and she was momentarily horrified that she could be so spontaneously uninhibited with this woman. Part of her screamed for her stop, to protect herself, that she was leaving herself so exposed.

She couldn't think about anything except the magic of Alex's fingers and the storm that seemed to be gathering within her, the storm that swelled until she thought she might explode. And then she did, crying out Alex's name as wave after wave of sensuous pleasure swept over her, her release leaving her tremblingly clinging to Alex's body.

As she quietened, Alex's mouth found hers. Just as suddenly, tears poured down Jo's cheeks and a wild sob caught in her throat.

"Darling?" Alex held Jo's face in her hands, her thumbs wiping against the dampness of her cheeks. "Did I hurt you?"

Jo quickly shook her head, taking hold of Alex's hand, placing soft fervent kisses in her palm. "No. No, you didn't hurt me. It's just that I've never felt so wonderful before. Oh, Alex. Thank you."

Alex laughed softly. "I think I should be thanking you, Jo." Her voice dropped impossibly deeper. "You're so incredibly, excitingly responsive. I want to start all over again."

And she did. This time her lips followed her

questing fingertips, and when her tongue found the tangled wetness Jo quivered anew. Her release this time took a little longer but still shook Jo with its intensity.

"I've never . . . I mean, it's never happened for me before," she told Alex. Alex raised her eyebrows. "Not like that."

"Not even on your own?"

Jo flushed and shook her head. "Sometimes it felt quite nice. I tried because Ben wanted me to, but I just seemed to get tense with embarrassment and it, well, sometimes it was painful." Jo stopped. "Was I embarrassing, Alex?" she asked softly, and Alex clutched her tightly to her.

"Not at all. You were simply breathtaking," Alex said against her earlobe. Jo shivered, luxuriating in the feel of Alex's body against her own.

Jo smiled lazily. "I dreamed it though," she said softly. Alex looked down at her. "Lately I've been dreaming more often. And the dreams included you."

Alex laughed. "So your subconscious was receiving my messages?"

"Loud and clear I think. But I was too slow to take heed. Until now." She reached up, ran a finger along the smoothness of Alex's jawline, up to her lips, rested on their softness. "And I'm so glad I did."

Desire rose again, and Jo's heartbeats tripped all over themselves. She wasn't close enough to Alex. And she wanted to give Alex the same pleasure. She swallowed nervously. Would she be able to?

"I want to make love to you, too, Alex," she said thickly.

"I was hoping you would," Alex said with a crooked smile. "And I do feel just a little over-dressed."

She stood up and slipped off her pants. Jo drank in the sight of her full curves, the dark curls between her firm thighs. Then Alex was sliding down beside Jo, her warm skin like smooth silk, sending tingles over Jo where their bodies touched.

"You feel so wonderful," Jo said against Alex's breast. When she took Alex's nipple into her mouth, Alex made a low, erotic noise deep in her throat.

Alex moved slightly, raising herself on one elbow, leaning across to kiss Jo again, and Jo responded, wrapping her arms around Alex's broad back, tenta-tively letting her fingers feel the softness of her flesh, the slight indentation of her backbone, found the dimples she'd seen in the photograph. Her hand slid around to Alex's side, over the swell of her hips, her waist, slowly moving upward until she cupped one of Alex's full breasts.

Breathing shallowly, Alex moved over Jo, her knee slipping between Jo's thighs. The dark triangle tickled Jo's skin as Alex rubbed herself against Jo's leg. She felt the dampness of her and heard Alex catch her breath.

"Touch me," Alex said unevenly.

Jo's free hand slid over Alex's hips, found the curls of hair, slipped into her wetness. "Am I . . . ? Tell me what to do," Jo begged.

"Just do what you're doing, what you feel like doing," Alex replied thickly, and Jo's lips returned to Alex's breast, her fingers matching Alex's movements, quickening her pace as Alex did.

171

Then Alex tensed, her fingers twisting in the sheets, and with a soft moan she collapsed onto the length of Jo's body.

Jo rubbed her back, murmured in her ear, drew in the mingled scent of their lovemaking.

Alex sighed softly and stretched out beside Jo. She closed her eyes, her breathing slowing. She was silent for so long Jo thought she had gone to sleep. Jo simply lay beside her, holding her, content to absorb the sensations of Alex's body joined with hers, wishing they could stay that way forever.

She'd never felt such closeness to anyone before. Her body burned with the wonder of the moment, with knowing her dreams had crystallized, merged with an incredible reality.

She'd definitely never felt like this with Ben. After Ben had climaxed he'd moved off her, rolled over, and gone to sleep.

Once, in the beginning, she'd tried to talk to him, create some bond between them, but he'd yawned and uninterestedly patted her leg, telling her just to enjoy it, that they didn't need to analyze it afterward. Jo's body moved slightly at the memory of her feeling of rejection.

"Jo?" Alex's deep voice sent different shivers over Jo's body.

"Mmm?"

Alex raised herself on one elbow. "Are you," she paused slightly, "all right?"

"Yes. Absolutely wonderful." She kissed Alex's smooth shoulder. "I guess I feel sort of shocked. That it was so good."

"Was that a vote of confidence?" Alex asked.

Jo looked up at her. "A hundred out of ten," she said with a smile.

Alex chuckled and sat up. "Would you like something to eat?"

"Only you."

Alex turned to look down at her, and Jo flushed.

"I'd like to kiss you, too, Alex," she said, hesitantly touching the curling dark hair.

Alex covered Jo's fingers with her own, held them there for a moment, then she leaned over to give Jo a quick kiss.

"I'd like you to, too," she said. "But in a while. I'm a little sensitive at the moment." She made a face. "Must be all the false alarms I've had these past few weeks. Seeing you looking all hot and bothered as you got undressed on the beach. Sharing your bed that night it rained and having you snuggle up to me. Now that was a masterful piece of self-restraint on my part. I can't believe you didn't feel me throbbing."

Jo bit off a chuckle. "Really?"

"Oh, yes," Alex said with feeling. "And then that kiss the other night. It's a wonder I haven't made tracks to a nunnery or taken a job in Antarctica or something."

"I'm sorry, Alex. Have I been a pain in the derriere?"

"I wouldn't quite call it the derriere," she said. "But you're getting close."

Jo laughed and then sobered. "Alex, when did you know you were gay?" she asked quietly.

Alex shrugged. "I can't say I woke up one morning and the knowledge hit me right between the

173

eyes. And I don't remember recognizing I was a lesbian when I was young. But I do know I felt different.

"Perhaps it was just not realizing there was a name for it. Who knows? I always felt sort of out of step. I was never comfortable with the idea of having a boyfriend and all that it entailed."

"But you got married," Jo reminded her, and Alex smiled crookedly again.

"Well, I did say I was young and foolish." She gave a soft laugh. "I guess it all came with a kind of misguided need to conform. I enjoyed the games the boys played, and they just treated me like one of them. That's how Rick and I noticed each other I suppose.

"We walked home from school together because we both went the same way. And when it came time for the school dance we took it for granted I'd go with him and he'd kiss me goodnight."

"How old were you then?"

"About fourteen or fifteen I think. And after that Rick took every opportunity to walk me past the creek. We'd slide down behind a bank and kiss some more." Alex picked up a strand of Jo's fair hair and let it slip through her fingers.

"Did you like it?"

Alex chuckled. "I kept going with him, so I couldn't have hated it. Looking back I think I saw it as some kind of symbol, that it showed the other kids I was the same as they were."

"And the sex part? Did you like that?" Jo flushed, watching Alex's face to see if she was offending her with her questions.

Alex's full mouth quirked. "The first time we did

it it was pretty disastrous. I was really tense because I thought someone might come along and catch us. We fumbled around for ages. When we finally hit the spot it hurt like hell and I cried out. Rick sprang off me in absolute terror, and that was the end of that. It took us months to brave another try."

"It hurt me too, the first time," Jo said quietly. Alex was silent for a moment before she tightened her arms around Jo and pulled her comfortingly close to her warm body.

"I've spoken to women who say they didn't feel any discomfort. I guess it depends on how relaxed you are, how aroused you are, and who's doing the arousing." Alex sighed, her hand absently rubbing Jo's bare arm. "I can't say I disliked having sex with Rick back then."

"I never got to like it," Jo admitted to Alex. "Ben said . . ." Jo swallowed. "He said I was probably frigid. I know I started to believe him. He got me books and I read about the earth moving and all that, but I think I wrote myself off as a failure as a mover and a shaker." Jo laughed self-consciously.

"Maybe Ben should have read a few books himself," Alex suggested.

Jo sighed. "Maybe."

"A lot of women find sex unsatisfying, Jo, straight and gay. As far as I'm concerned it's the love, the closeness that comes with it, that counts as the bottom line.

"I never found that closeness with Rick. Nor did I find the physical act all that satisfying with him. Not like I do with a woman." She kissed Jo softly on the nose. Jo's throat tightened, heat rising over her again.

"I think we can put the idea that you're frigid to rest, don't you?" Alex added softly.

"Do you think so?"

"Absolutely."

Jo glanced at Alex and then away. "How did you first realize you were attracted to women?"

"A particular woman," Alex said flatly. Something stirred painfully in the region of Jo's heart at the bleakness of Alex's tone.

She wanted to pull Alex to her, too, take away what was obviously a deep hurt.

Then Alex sighed, her breath stirring Jo's hair, teasing the curve of her cheek.

"I met Jean when I'd been in Brisbane for nearly a year," Alex said at last. "I had a job in a picture framing shop, and Jean came in to get some of her photographs framed. Her work was great, and I exclaimed over them, told her I was interested in photography. She invited me along on a trip to Binna Burra, photographing the rain forest."

"What was she like?"

"She was in her early forties, very fit, strong body, beautiful face. She taught me everything I know about taking photos and processing and printing. I fell for her like a ton of bricks. She took that photo," Alex indicated the print on the wall, "and the one downstairs. Then she taught me all about making love. The first time made me realize just what had been missing from my life, all my life."

I feel like that when you kiss me, Jo wanted to cry out to Alex, but she bit her lip, something holding her back. "Why did you break up?" she asked tentatively.

"Another eager twenty-year-old who was interested in photography came along," Alex said levelly.

"Oh," Jo murmured inadequately.

"It was pretty devastating. Considering it came out that there had been a couple of others over the years that I didn't know about. I challenged her about what I considered to be our commitment to each other. We couldn't find any common ground so we sold our house and went our separate ways. That's when I came up here."

"Has there been anyone else since then?"

Alex was silent for a moment. "No one special. After Jean I didn't feel I wanted to get into any heavy relationships. Too much wear and tear. Or maybe too much pain, too little gain," she finished lightly.

Jo felt the heaviness of what Alex had left unspoken. Alex wasn't interested in another relationship.

So what did Alex feel toward the inexperienced, totally unspectacular little nobody that Jo saw herself as? She desperately wanted to ask her. Yet she knew she couldn't bear to hear the answer, not in so many cold, clear words.

"What about you?" Alex asked then. "I take it you never had any secret dreams about making love to a woman?"

Jo drew her tortured thoughts back from the dark place to which they'd strayed. "No. I don't think so. Or to a man. I never seemed to be able to mix very well with anyone actually.

"When I was growing up we were never in one place long enough for me to feel comfortable with the girls, let alone the boys." Jo shrugged. "But I do remember preferring to be with women at work. For what that's worth. I was painfully shy anyway. I think when Ben showed an interest in me I was flattered and probably simply relieved.

"But I never considered" — she swallowed — "I don't think I even knew the word *lesbian* until after I was married. So I can't say I was ever physically attracted to a woman. Until I met you."

The words hung in the air, seemed to Jo to ricochet above their heads. She waited for them to fall, crushing her beneath them.

"Well now." Alex ran her fingertip over Jo's shoulder, down her arm. "May I say I'm more than pleased that you are. There's nothing like a little physical attraction to set the ball rolling." She grimaced. "I'll rephrase that. There's nothing like a little physical attraction to, let me see . . ." Her fingertip continued its seductive course, crossed from Jo's arm to her stomach, circled her navel, slowly slid upward over Jo's breast, to tease its rosy peak. Jo moaned thickly.

"To hit the right spot," Alex breathed into Jo's ear, and then her lips were covering Jo's and Jo lost everything. Time. Place. Space. There was only Alex.

Some time later they reluctantly drew apart.

"Thanks for not giving up on me," Jo said a little breathlessly.

"I'll admit I kept telling myself not to be a fool, not to forget the other Farmer Golden Rule."

Jo raised her eyebrows. "Besides not making love to inebriated women?"

"Yes. Farmer Golden Rule Number Two. Not to sleep with straight women."

"I think my straight days are well and truly over," Jo said sincerely. When Alex frowned, Jo sat up. "What's the matter?" she asked.

Alex sighed. "Jo. Don't burn all your bridges. Not now. Not in the aftermath of great sex. A lifestyle is more than sex. That's a big part, I'll admit, the attraction and everything. But you have to live in a world that doesn't exactly smile down on you with approving benevolence."

"I know that, Alex. But you don't have to wear a sign either, do you? I mean, no one needs to know if you don't want to tell them. You never told me, not in so many words."

"Perhaps I didn't. But I don't actively hide the fact that I'm a lesbian. What I'm saying is, it's far more complicated than just deciding you want to sleep with a woman. And all that's on top of the usual difficulties that come with sorting out a relationship. Like whether or not you both want the same sort of commitment."

Jo swallowed. What was Alex telling her? Not to put too much importance on this? That good sex didn't mean everlasting love? That this was great for now but not something she wanted to give any permanence to? Hadn't Alex intimated she wasn't looking for another involvement?

"You stay there, and I'll make us a sandwich." Alex stood up. "Are you as famished as I am?"

Jo nodded and Alex picked up her shirt, leaving Jo with a hundred conflicting emotions.

They made love again later, and Jo could only marvel at her responses, her lack of inhibitions with Alex, and Alex's responses to her. They lay together, bodies entwined, and as they fell asleep in each other's arms, Jo pushed her feelings of disquiet out of her mind.

CHAPTER FIFTEEN

Sitting alone in her flat the next afternoon, Jo couldn't prevent those same feelings of uneasiness returning to unsettle her. The sun had been shining when they'd waked this morning, but Alex's words hadn't really reassured Jo.

Alex had glanced at the bedside clock and groaned. "Oh, no. I'll have to get going." She turned to Jo, her eyes running over Jo's naked body pressed against hers.

"Do we have to get up?" Jo asked, her lips

tasting a spot above Alex's left breast. Alex groaned again.

"I have to. I have another appointment with my accountant in Brisbane in about an hour and a half."

"You can't cancel it?" Jo suggested.

Alex shook her head. "Not at this time of year. I was lucky to get this appointment. It's to finalize my income tax." She pushed herself into a sitting position. "I can't believe I'm going to be talking tax when I want to be making love with you."

Jo laughed softly, awed at the wonder of Alex's sensual body as she walked into the en suite. She would have liked to make love with Alex again, too. Her body tingled at the mere thought.

And from there Jo again began to consider just what Alex now expected of her. Did she go home and wait for Alex to call her when she was free?

Alex appeared in the doorway. "We can conserve water and shower together," she suggested with a smile that faltered a little at Jo's uncertain expression. "What's the matter?" She came back and stood by the bed. "Look, I'm really sorry about today, Jo, but I do have to go down to Brisbane."

"Oh, no. I know you have. It's not that. I was just, well, wondering. About us." Jo couldn't meet Alex's eyes for fear of what she'd see there.

Alex sighed. "There's no problem, Jo. I realize you probably feel you don't want to get involved so soon, what with your divorce. I felt the same when I broke up with Jean. You need time to find yourself, to be yourself. And apart from you and me, this will be radically changing your whole lifestyle as well.

Perhaps it might be better for both of us if we take it slowly."

"You mean, no strings attached?" Jo asked in a thin voice.

Alex stood up. "Well, yes," she said lightly and walked back toward the bathroom.

Jo lay there for long moments, feeling lost and unsure, and then she slowly followed Alex.

She stood watching the curve of Alex's body behind the glass shower door, and her heart constricted painfully. She wanted nothing more than to be with Alex, but it seemed Alex didn't need such an intense involvement.

"Are you coming in?" Alex's deep voice drew her out of her abject misery. Jo walked forward, feeling a rush of bittersweet emotion as Alex drew her beneath the cool water and ran her wet, soapy hands over Jo's immediately responsive body.

They made love under the teasing water jets, Alex making Jo cry out with pleasure. As a result they spent far too long in the shower. After a quick breakfast, Alex rode off to Brisbane on her motorcycle while Jo drove home to her flat.

And Jo had been sitting despondently, wondering what to do. Should she try to explain to Alex how she felt? Or would Alex then find some reason for extricating herself from a situation she found too stifling?

Jo sighed, feeling desperately naive. She'd simply had no experience in such things, and she didn't quite know what the protocol was. She grimaced. Or if there was such a thing. It was all so complicated.

The thought of losing Alex didn't bear thinking about but she suspected she'd make a king-size mess of it if she tried to express her feelings. She was still trying to decide what she'd say to Alex when Mike Craven poked his head in her open door.

"Hi!" he said tentatively. "I saw your car and knew you must be back."

"I got back before lunch."

"Over your headache?"

"Yes. Thanks."

An uncomfortable silence fell, and Jo took a steadying breath. Alex or no Alex she knew she couldn't be less than honest with Mike.

"I spent the night with," she paused just slightly, "a friend."

"I see." Mike held her gaze. "A special friend?" he asked lightly, and Jo nodded.

"Yes. Pretty special."

Mike nodded too. "I guess you don't want to go for a drive up the coast this afternoon then."

"I'm sorry, Mike. No." She looked at her wrist-watch. "I was going out in half an hour or so anyway."

"Okay." He started to go and then turned back toward her. "I just wanted to say I really appreciated your listening to my sad story the other night. I needed to talk. And if I can ever do the same for you, well, my shoulder's here."

"Thanks, Mike. I'll remember that."

He smiled. "No worries. I hope you'll be happy, Jo. Really."

"You too, Mike," she said sincerely.

He gave a crooked smile and walked away.

Jo crossed slowly over to close the door. With

shaky resolve she changed into a fresh pair of shorts and a T-shirt and went out to the car.

Once again she took the road toward Maleny. She recalled her agitation yesterday over her need to salvage her friendship with Alex, rethink the timbre of that friendship. Friendship? Jo shivered slightly, responsively. They were certainly now far more than friends.

Jo's whole life had changed so much. And it might very well change again, she reminded herself, after she'd seen Alex. But she had to take this chance. She didn't want a covert affair.

Her heartbeats accelerated as she negotiated the steep driveway and pulled up in front of Alex's house. The motorcycle was under the carport so she knew Alex was back from Brisbane. But parked beside the bike was a dark, expensive-looking convertible, a BMW, Jo realized on closer inspection. Alex must have visitors. Her heart sank a little. Selfishly she'd wanted Alex to herself.

Should she go inside? Would Alex want her to? Jo sat there, unable to move, until she took herself firmly to task. She had changed, hadn't she? She was taking charge of herself, her life. She climbed out of the car and knocked firmly on the door.

Alex opened it almost immediately. "I was going to phone you."

"I should have called —" Jo began at the same time, and Alex smiled faintly. Jo's knees went weak at the rush of emotion just seeing Alex evoked inside her.

"Alex?" A husky, melodic voice came from inside the house, and Jo glanced quickly at Alex.

"Go on in, Jo," she said softly after a moment,

standing back for Jo to enter. Jo walked uncertainly past her, into the living room.

A dark-haired woman uncoiled herself from her position on the couch. She was tall and very attractive in a cool sort of way, and Jo could only admire her perfect control and poise.

The woman wore dark Garbo pants and a light blouse, the long full sleeves gathered around wide cuffs at her wrists. The top buttons on the front of the shirt were unbuttoned to reveal her cleavage, and a gold pendant rested in the valley between her breasts. Jo was sure she could see the dark shadow of the woman's nipples through the thin material and she hurriedly raised her eyes to the woman's face.

She was beautifully made up, and her dark hair was pulled back in a neat chignon. Delicate gold earrings dangled from her ears. She was the most elegant woman Jo had seen in her life.

Jo paused, feeling gauche and untidy in her cotton shorts and oversize T-shirt. She felt the woman taking in every inch of her appearance, and she had to prevent herself from straightening her shirt, fiddling with her hair.

"Well, Alex." The woman smiled. "Aren't you going to introduce me to your young friend?"

"Of course." Alex came forward then. "This is Jo Creighton. Jo, meet Jean Lansing."

Jean? Was this the woman Alex had been in love with? Her gaze flicked to Alex, but she could glean nothing from the shuttered expression on Alex's face.

But hadn't Alex said Jean was in her forties when they met? That had been seventeen years ago and would put this woman in her late fifties. Yet she barely looked fifteen years younger than that.

Jo's heart sank. The woman who held out her perfectly manicured hand was everything that Jo could never be.

"A very spartan introduction, Alex," Jean commented and smiled again at Jo. "I'm an old friend of Alex's from Brisbane. We go way back."

"Hello." Jo found her voice and muttered inanely, feeling herself begin to flush as a heavy silence fell.

"Alex was just making a cup of tea," Jean put in. "Would you like a cup, Jo?" she asked graciously, sitting herself back down on the couch and crossing one long leg gracefully over the other.

Jo glanced at Alex to see her move slightly with uncharacteristic indecision. Jo didn't know what to do, couldn't begin to decide whether Alex wanted her to go or stay.

"Oh, no. Thank you," she got out. "I didn't realize Alex had visitors. I think perhaps I should be going."

"No." Alex and Jean said in unison, and Alex seemed to gather herself together.

"No, you don't have to go, Jo." She lightly touched Jo's arm, a movement Jo saw didn't go unnoticed by the older woman. "I've made the tea. I'll pour you a cup. Okay?"

"All right," Jo agreed. Alex gave her a quick smile as she crossed to the kitchen.

"Why don't you make yourself comfortable." Jean patted the couch beside her.

Jo sat down gingerly and made herself lean back into the soft cushions. Her gaze was again drawn to the silhouette of Jean's nipples, and she flushed with embarrassment when she looked up and realized Jean was quite aware of her scrutiny.

"Well, now. Tell me all about yourself, Jo," Jean continued, a small smile playing around her mouth. "How long have you and Alex," she paused almost imperceptibly, "known each other?"

"Not very long, actually." Jo tried to relax her tensed muscles. "A few weeks." A lifetime, Jo wanted to add.

"And what do you do?"

"Do? Oh, my job you mean?" Jo swallowed her nervousness. "I work in a bank, but I'm up here on holiday."

"Ah. A quaint little place, isn't it? Although a little too arty for me." Jean's long fingers brushed at an imaginary speck of dust on her slacks.

"The galleries seem to do a very brisk trade in artwork," Jo ventured and Jean smiled.

"I'm sure they do, with the tourists."

"Alex does well with her cards," Jo plowed on with what was becoming a stilted conversation.

"Her cards?" Jean raised her fine brows.

"I use some of my photographs on greeting cards and the gift shops sell them," Alex explained as she rejoined them.

"I see." Jean laughed. "Very perspicacious, my dear."

Alex set the tray of cups on the coffee table.

"Alex won a few prizes with her photographs at a craft show just recently," Jo told Jean.

"Alex always was very talented, and a willing pupil," Jean added softly, her eyes on Alex's back as she bent over the teacups.

188

"She got a first with one of her nature ones and a second with the portrait she took of me." Jo couldn't seem to stop herself babbling on.

Jean's dark eyes ran over Jo, and her lips twisted as Alex passed her her tea. "So the circle keeps on turning," she murmured, and Jo was sure light color flooded Alex's face. "You'll have to take me down to your studio and show me some of your recent work, love."

Alex made no comment as she passed Jo her cup without meeting her eyes.

"Mmm." Jean took an appreciative sip of her tea. "Just the way I like it. You always could make a marvelous cuppa."

Alex sat in the single chair, and Jo watched Alex's face, trying to read Alex's reactions to this woman's teasing innuendos. Was there still something between Alex and Jean? Alex had said her last relationship was over, but maybe Alex was still in love with this beautiful woman. How could Alex not be?

A shaft of pain stabbed and settled in the region of Jo's heart, and she felt tears sting her eyes. She swallowed convulsively and took a steadying breath. Surely Alex would have told her, wouldn't have taken Jo to bed if . . . But maybe they had an open relationship.

"You're a photographer, too, aren't you?" Jo forced herself to ask the older woman.

"Yes, I am. In fact I suppose you could say I taught Alex all she knows. About photography," she added enigmatically.

"I've seen the photos you took of her," Jo continued with more composure than she was feeling. "That one on the wall and the one upstairs."

Jean's eyes narrowed, and Jo flushed again.

"They're quite wonderful."

"Thank you." Jean inclined her head. "I especially like the one upstairs, don't you?"

The photograph was etched in Jo's mind. She knew every sensuous line of Alex's body. She swallowed, her face beginning to burn. "Actually, I saw it when Alex, when I . . . One night when I'd had too much to drink Alex kindly let me sleep it off."

Jo could have bitten her tongue. Why had she let this woman goad her into trying to justify the fact that she'd been in Alex's bedroom? Jo blushed again.

"Oh, yes. Alex was always kind." Jean took another sip of her tea.

"Jean!" Alex said quietly, and the other woman looked up blandly.

"Well, you are. Many's the time —" she began but Alex didn't allow her to continue.

"Jean's come up to do a photographic series on the Woodford-Maleny Folk Festival this weekend," Alex said quickly to Jo. "I'd forgotten it was on. You might like to go while you're here, Jo. It's quite an interesting few days."

While you're here? The words echoed in Jo's head. What was Alex saying?

"It seemed like an excellent opportunity to catch up with my old friend. Combine a little business with a lot of pleasure," Jean added, and that same heavy silence fell again.

"I don't believe you told me how you met Alex," Jean added, settling back into the sofa. She was a picture of self-confidence and was totally in command of the situation, something Jo was far from feeling.

"We met when I was doing some sketching. I trespassed on Alex's land, and she took me sternly to task." Jo tried to keep her tone light.

"Alex did?" Jean laughed. "You must have got under her skin."

"I was having a bad day," Alex cut in quickly. "So what basic theme will you be using for your series on the festival, Jean?" she asked, pointedly changing the subject. The older woman made a face at her and set down her teacup.

"I want to get some earthy shots, focusing on the women, of course. I hear this year there'll be a couple of well-known American performers joining our own Judy Small. I was hoping you might come along, Alex, help me with my gear, like old times," Jean finished.

"What about Marnie? Doesn't she usually do that?" Alex asked, her voice carefully noncommittal.

Jean's dark eyes narrowed fractionally and she gave Alex a crooked smile. "Marnie isn't with me any more."

"I see." Alex was apparently finding the dregs of her teacup quite fascinating.

Jo's stomach twisted at the sudden increase in the heavy tension in the room, and she made herself stand up. "I think I should be going," she said, replacing her empty cup on the tray. "Thanks for the tea, Alex. It was nice to meet you, Jean."

The other woman inclined her head. "Likewise, Jo," she said, smiling her perfect smile.

Jo glanced quickly at Alex, swallowed the lump that had lodged painfully in her throat. Was Alex just going to let her go?

CHAPTER SIXTEEN

"I'll see you later, Alex." Jo turned, found the door, and stepped outside.

"Jo. Wait."

Alex's voice halted her, and Jo turned slightly, her hand clutching at the car for support.

"Jo, I'm sorry." Alex moved around the car, took hold of Jo's hand, laced her fingers with Jo's. The touch of Alex's hand sparked a rush of wanting that left Jo weak.

"I'll call you soon. Okay?" Alex said softly, and Jo nodded, unable to speak.

Alex released her hand, and Jo climbed into her car and set off on the lonely drive home. She spent the rest of the afternoon prowling about her flat trying to tell herself she wasn't just waiting for the phone to ring.

When it did she was momentarily paralyzed then almost dropped the receiver in her haste.

"Jo? Hi! It's Alex."

As if Jo needed Alex to tell her that. "Hello," she said carefully.

"I'm sorry I haven't rung sooner. How are you?" Her voice dropped, its intimate tone playing over Jo, raising light goose bumps along her arms.

"I'm fine." She swallowed. "Have you had a nice afternoon catching up with your friend?"

"Yes. And no. Look, Jo. I'm sorry, but I'm going to be tied up for a few days. As Jean said, she wants to do part of the series featuring the women involved in the preparations, the lead up to the festival, that sort of stuff, and she wants me to give her a hand."

Jo made an effort to relax her fingers where her knuckles were turning white clutching the phone. "I see," she said carefully. "How long will she be here?"

"Until after the festival." Alex paused. "Would you like to come along?"

"With you and Jean?"

"Yes."

Jo swallowed. "I'd only get in the way if you're working. You'd be better off on your own. But I might come down and have a look at it," she added quickly to show Alex she wasn't upset over the situation, that she was making no demands on her.

"I think you'd enjoy it. There's a very good concert on the last day," Alex was saying.

"Where's Jean staying?" Jo asked before she could stop herself.

Alex paused again. "Here with me," Alex replied evenly.

"Oh." An uncharacteristic surge of jealousy clutched at Jo, and she took a steadying breath.

"I've offered Jean the use of my darkroom, so it will be more convenient."

"You don't have to explain, Alex," Jo said softly.

"I know I don't have to. But I wanted to." Alex sighed. "Bear with me on this, Jo. Please. And I'll be in touch soon. Okay?"

"All right. Good-bye, Alex." She replaced the receiver as tears rose to catch painfully in her throat.

Jo barely slept that night, torturing herself with thoughts of Alex and Jean, and next day she languished in her small flat. She kept telling herself she wasn't a spineless little wimp any more, that she had to get on with her life.

Yet she tormented herself with the idea that maybe seeing Jean again had rekindled Alex's old love. Why wouldn't Alex be attracted to such a beautiful, self-possessed, obviously successful woman?

Jo wished now that she had asked Alex more about her first love. She did recall the sadness on Alex's face when they were driving down to Caloundra and Alex had spoken of her broken relationship. Only back then Jo had thought Alex was talking about a man. She could almost laugh at her preconceived thoughts. How naive she'd been. Still was, she reminded herself.

And she was a fool. Why hadn't she told Alex how she'd felt the other morning?

When Alex suggested they shouldn't get carried away on the aftermath of great sex, why hadn't she told Alex how she felt? That she'd fallen in love with her, that it hadn't happened just because of the great sex, but that it had been happening almost from the moment she'd seen her standing on the track like a gorgeous, desirable, wonderful Valkyrie.

Or perhaps sooner. In her dreams.

And now she suspected it was too late.

Jo was staring disinterestedly at her sketches when there was a knock on her open door. She turned, blinked in the afternoon light, scarcely believing Alex could be there.

"I remembered about the bell this time. Thought I'd let that particular sleeping dog lie," Alex said with a crooked grin. "Can I come in?"

Jo stood back, and Alex stepped inside. She slowly closed the door behind her, leaned back against it, her hand still on the doorknob as though she'd forgotten to let it go. Her eyes met Jo's and Jo let out the breath she'd been holding, wondering if her suddenly weak knees were going to hold her.

Then Alex moved, took Jo in her arms, and Jo clung to her, kissing her feverishly, until they drew breathlessly apart.

"Well!" Alex sighed appreciatively. "Does that mean you missed me?"

Jo tried to laugh, but it choked off and Alex looked down at her in concern. "I thought perhaps I wouldn't see you again," she said softly, and Alex murmured low in her throat.

"Oh, Jo. I'm sorry. Of all the times Jean could

pick to drop in. She's never been up here before. It was the very worst bad timing."

Jo swallowed, made herself walk a few paces from Alex. "She's very attractive."

"Yes, she is. And she seems to get more attractive as she gets older. Which hardly seems fair." Alex grimaced. "But all that aside, I needed to talk to you."

Alex subsided onto the couch, and Jo sank into the chair opposite her.

"I'm sorry Jean was there when you called. I would have preferred to be alone with you. I wanted to talk," Alex began.

"I did, too," Jo said. "There were things I felt I needed to say." Her words hung heavily in the air for immeasurable moments, and Alex seemed to tense.

"There were? Well, do you want to tell me now?"

Jo swallowed. "You may not want to hear this, Alex, not now that Jean's here."

"Jean's not a part of my life any more, Jo. At least, not the way you mean," Alex said softly. "That's what I came over to explain to you. About Jean."

"You don't have to, Alex. I know I have no right to . . ."

"Yes, you do. And I want you to know." Alex sighed. "I still care about Jean."

A pain began in Jo's chest, and she took a steadying breath.

"Jean was such a big part of my life after my son's death, my divorce. She brought me back to life emotionally. We were together for so many years, and even when I found out she wasn't as committed to our relationship as I was, I wanted to remain friends

197

with her. That's why I left her when I did, before even that friendship died. But I'm not in love with her, Jo. She knows that, too."

Jo's numbed heart gave a hopeful flutter. Did that mean Alex might . . . ?

"I don't want to cut Jean out of my life, but I also don't expect you to want to include her in yours."

"You don't want to get back together with her then?" Jo asked tentatively.

Alex shook her head. "No. Our relationship was over when I found out that Jean enjoyed playing the field behind my back. Maybe before then, I don't know. I do know I felt absolutely betrayed. When I make a commitment I do just that, and I expect my partner to do the same. Jean has different ideas, and it took me a long time to realize that. Okay?"

Jo nodded.

"So. That's what I wanted to say. Now it's your turn," Alex said carefully.

Jo looked seriously at Alex. "As I said, you may not want to hear it, Alex."

"Maybe not, but you said you needed to say it." Alex rested her elbow on the arm of the couch, rubbed at her bottom lip with her thumb.

Jo felt the nervous flutter of her heart in her chest. "When I first met you, even though you scared the living daylights out of me, I couldn't get you out of my mind." She smiled faintly. "I see now there was always something different about my feelings for you, right from the start, but I never recognized them for what they were. I just knew I liked being with you, I guess. That's never happened to me before. With anyone.

"I wanted to explain to you how I . . ." Jo stopped, her throat dry. "When we made love. Before that. And afterward. I'd never felt quite that way before. The way you made me feel."

Jo looked at Alex, and she felt as though she was again drowning in the dark intensity of her steady gaze. She drew courage from what she saw reflected in Alex's eyes.

"I love you, Alex," she said huskily. "My feelings for you have made me whole somehow. It's as though someone turned on a light inside me, deep inside me, or shuffled the pieces of the jigsaw that's me and the pieces have all fallen together in the right place."

The words came bubbling out, free now, and Jo rushed on. "I don't know how you feel about living with someone, and I won't ask that if it's not what you want. I respect that you may not want to take another chance. But I want to be near you.

"So I thought, as I'd already put in for a transfer before I left, I might ask to be moved to a branch of the bank somewhere up on the North Coast, and then we could perhaps see each other sometimes.

"I only know that when I'm not with you I feel only half alive," Jo finished, her voice breaking.

Alex shook her head. "Jo, right now all I want to do is put my arms around you, hold you to me, never let you go. But I want to be fair to you, too. I want you to be absolutely sure you know exactly what you're getting yourself into."

Jo started to speak, but Alex held up her hand.

"No. Let me get this out. While I still can." She gave a crooked smile. "At the moment we probably both feel we could exist only for each other, cocooned away from other people, from everything, but it doesn't work that way in the real world.

"If you take this step you'll be shunned by some, looked upon as a freak by others. You'll lose friends. And to tell you the truth," Alex wiped a shaking hand across her brow, "I don't think I could take it now if you . . . if after a while you decided to change your mind."

Jo moved out of her chair, knelt in front of Alex and took her hands. "I'll never do that. Even if you send me away. I've finally found myself, the real me, and I've never known such inner peace and strength.

"I know it won't be easy. I have parents, a family who loves me. I can't begin to imagine how they'll react. I hope they'll continue to care about me. But Alex, that doesn't matter as much as you and me. I never believed I could feel so loving. Or so loved." Her eyes met Alex's. "Do you love me, Alex?"

"More than I thought it was possible to love anyone again," she said simply and reached out, slowly pulling Jo into her arms. And Jo went willingly.

They gazed into each other's eyes, and Alex smiled, uncharacteristically uncertain.

"This is another last chance, Jo. To change your mind," she added with a wry smile as she drew Jo against her. "Because once I get you in my arms again, I don't ever intend to let you go."

Jo delighted in the softness of Alex's body. "You'll have to drive me away."

Their kiss was long and lingeringly sweet. When

Jo drew back, she had to swallow the tears that threatened to choke her. "The other morning when I said no strings attached and you agreed, I thought I'd die," she said.

Alex raised her eyes in mock exasperation. "I thought that was what you wanted to hear. It took all my self-control to agree with that, Jo. I didn't want to stifle you, frighten you off. Not when I finally had you in my arms."

"You were interested in me all along then?" Jo asked lightly.

Alex gave her a quick hard kiss. "Why do you think I went back to where you were sketching each day in the hope that you'd be there? I was running twice every day instead of a grudging three times a week. Now if that's not interest I don't know what is." Alex sobered, ran a light finger over Jo's cheek.

"That first day when I was so exasperated, well, I'd had a call from Jean." Alex grimaced. "Jean again. She rang, to quote her, just to touch base. She'd probably contacted me about three times since we separated. Why she chose that day I'll never know. Probably the same reason she turned up here this week." Alex shook her head.

"But anyway, Jean knows which buttons to press with me, and after her call let's just say I wasn't feeling particularly appreciative of the world in general.

"I was walking my irritation off, and then I came upon you sitting there." Alex gently stroked the smooth skin of Jo's arm. "I'm not usually so gung-ho, but when you turned around something inside me instinctively knew my life would never be quite the same. I told myself I was a fool to even contemplate starting all over again, maybe going through the same pain.

"But after I left you I couldn't get you out of my mind." Alex shook her head. "I couldn't stop myself going back the next morning. Of course, you weren't there, and I thought I'd frightened you off."

"You very nearly did," Jo told her, and the corner of Alex's mouth twisted self-derisively.

"Then I saw you in the craft shop," she continued, "and I couldn't believe my good luck. And when I found myself looking to see if you had on a wedding ring, I knew I was in big trouble. I felt like a schoolkid, all tongue-tied and gauche."

"It certainly didn't show."

"Believe it, Jo. It's true," Alex said sincerely. "I even delved to find out who you were buying my card for. I thought it might be a boyfriend."

"Bet you were relieved when I said it was for my sister-in-law," Jo teased.

Alex made a face. "Well, even after that bit of detective work, my relief was pretty short-lived. Just when I thought you might be looking at me favorably, you mentioned building a house with Ben. Now I could not stretch my imagination to seeing you involved with a woman called Ben."

Jo laughed delightedly.

"So. You then told me you and Ben were divorcing and I got all relieved again. Until old tall, blond, and good-looking came on the scene. I spent the worst night of my life the night you went out with him." She pursed her lips in mock disapproval. "Honestly, I can see I'm going to have my hands full in the future, deflecting all these would-be romeos."

"You'll have no worries there, Alex." Jo chuckled. "As my revolting ex-husband-to-be said, I think you've tickled my fancy."

Alex raised her eyebrows. "I don't think I want to know why, and in relation to what, he said that."

"Believe me, you don't. I'm sorry Ben was so rude to you. And that I didn't react more positively. I was so surprised to see you there that by the time I'd recovered Ben was all wound up being obnoxious."

Alex gave a short laugh. "Now we've both apologized for our ex-partners."

"I guess it makes a change from me apologizing *to* mine," Jo remarked derisively.

"Was he always such a pain?" Alex asked sympathetically.

Jo shrugged. "I think he was. But, as I said, I was in such a dream those years of my marriage." She shrugged. "Looking back I don't understand why I married him. Everyone said he was charming, ambitious, good-looking, and I guess I was flattered he took an interest in me. It all seems like a fantasy now."

Jo sighed. "I used to wish that the world had ended on my wedding day, that I could have taken the euphoria of the ceremony, the reception, into eternity. Because the rest was a disaster."

"It was that bad?" Alex asked softly.

Jo nodded. "I was a virgin until my wedding night. One of the few left in captivity." She gave a mirthless laugh. "If I'd given in to Ben before we were married I know I would never have gone through with the wedding."

"Oh, Jo." Alex tenderly caressed Jo's back.

"I'm just glad all that, with Ben, is behind me."

"I am, too, but for different reasons," Alex said.

"The other morning, after we made love, I wasn't so sure you were," Jo said with feeling.

"I want to apologize about that." Alex's hands cupped Jo's face. "It's been so long since my first relationship with a woman and my life fell into place. I should have seen it from your side, should have remembered how frightening, how exciting it all was. Because I do remember. I've had all these years for it to become just a part of my life, and I'd forgotten how initially it's just about the sole focus of your existence.

"And I suppose I was uncertain, too. I knew how I felt about you, Jo, but I was also afraid to get involved again."

Jo shook her head. "I just can't believe you'd notice me. I'm so run-of-the-mill, fade-into-the-background. Ben always —"

Alex put her fingers to Jo's lips. "Do you admire Ben's actions this past year or so?" she asked.

Jo shook her head. "Of course not. As far as I'm concerned he has no integrity, no honor. Ben's totally self-absorbed."

"Then don't give anything he's said any credence." Alex's dark eyes looked levelly into Jo's gray ones. "I love you, Jo. The way you lift your chin when you're taking a stand. The pleasure you get from everything. For a million reasons.

"I want us to be together, but I think we should take it slowly, get to know each other better. And I want you to have an open door if you need an escape."

Jo raised her eyes toward the ceiling and appealed

to who or whatever was listening. "After all this she thinks I need an escape? Give me strength."

"I'm only thinking that this is all so new to you. If you want to change your mind —"

"I know what you're trying to say, Alex, but I don't think I'll be doing that somehow." Jo gave a self-derisive laugh. "It may be new to the conscious me, but my dreams have been trying to tell me all this for ages, and more forcefully recently.

"I think the realization has been dancing about in the back of my mind for years, in some form or other. I feel such wonder, such relief that it's finally taken shape. And that you were my dream lover."

"I am, too," Alex said with feeling and kissed Jo tenderly.

Jo murmured appreciatively. "Who would have thought that first day that you and I would have . . . ? What do you think would have happened if you'd actually told me you were a lesbian right in the beginning?"

"As in, 'Hello. I'm Alex Farmer. I'm a lesbian and have licentious designs upon your beautiful body.' "

Jo laughed. "Something like that."

"You'd have run a mile, Jo Creighton." Alex stated. "As a matter of fact, when you did find out you ran to Maleny. Remember?"

"I was such a fool." Jo gazed into Alex's eyes. "But I did run back pretty quickly if you'll recall."

"While I spent an hour imagining the worst." Alex kissed her again, and they clung to each other until eventually Alex stirred. "We've been talking so long the sun's completely gone."

"Do you think Jean will be worried about you?

Alex gave a soft laugh. "She probably hasn't

noticed I've gone. I introduced her to an eager young photographer, a long-legged blond, who begged to take over my job as Jean's assistant. I gave in graciously and tried not to let it show how ecstatic I was to get away to see you."

"You were?" Jo asked shyly.

"I most definitely was.

"Jean won't be missing you then?"

"I don't think so somehow. She'll be too engrossed in her latest conquest. So can I beg a meal and a bed?"

Jo paused to consider. "Oh, I think the bed can be arranged. As to the meal, you'll have to take pot-luck."

"Then perhaps we could test out that old adage," Alex suggested huskily.

Jo watched Alex's eyes darken and her heartbeats fell all over themselves. "What old adage is that?"

"The one about being able to live on love alone." Alex clarified.

"Love? Now wasn't that what was on the menu the other night?"

"I believe so," Alex murmured, her breath teasing Jo's sensitive earlobe. "Special of the Day. Well, the night actually."

"Then can I order more of the same?"

"You're not tired of it?"

"Oh, no. I've just developed the taste for it. And that pun was definitely intended." She gave a soft chuckle and lifted Alex's hand, taking one of Alex's fingers into her mouth, sucking it sensually.

"Mmm. In fact," Jo struck a pose of exaggerated contemplation, "I think I'll make it my staple diet. What do you think?"

Alex gave a soft, so arousing laugh. "I knew you were my kind of woman the minute I saw you." She gently laid Jo back along the couch, moving her body over Jo's. "And tonight I think we might even have dessert."

About the Author

Lyn Denison was born in Brisbane, the capital city of Queensland, Australia's Sunshine State. She was a librarian until she became a full-time writer. She loves reading, cross-stitch, travel, modern country music, line dancing, and her partner of nine years—not necessarily in that order. She lives with her partner in a colonial worker's cottage, which they have renovated, in a historic suburb near Brisbane's city center.